Bedside manners

BEDSIDE manners

Luisa Valenzuela

Translated by
Margaret Jull Costa

HIGH RISK
BOOKS

LONDON / NEW YORK

Library of Congress Cataloging-in-Publication Data

Valenzuela, Luisa, 1938–
[Realidad nacional desde la cama. English]
Bedside manners / Luisa Valenzuela.—1st U.S. ed.
    p.   cm.
ISBN 1–85242–313–7
I. Title
PQ7798.32.A48R4313   1994
863—dc20   94–28946
                                                CIP

A CIP record for this book can be obtained from the
British Library on request

First published in 1990 as *Realidad nacional desde la cama* by Grupo Editor
Latinoamericano S.R.L., Buenos Aires, Argentina

This edition first published in 1995 by
High Risk Books/Serpent's Tail
4 Blackstock Mews, London N4 2BT
and 401 West Broadway #1, New York, NY 10012

Cover design by Rex Ray
Set in 11/15 pt Janson by Intype, London
Printed in Finland by Werner Söderström Oy

1

Suspecting nothing of the superimposition of different planes of reality, unaware of the existence of the military camp or the shanty town, a woman has gone to seek refuge in a certain far-flung country club.

She's alone because she wants to be or because she doesn't feel like company and has taken to conducting long internal monologues purely for her own amusement. She tells herself for example:

I was born under the sign of Question the way others are born under the sign of Capricorn or Leo, which is not to say that I'm any more inclined than others to doubt or self-doubt, but I know what true ambivalence is. My ascendant is in Eyes, a dual sign, like Tits or Testes or Twin Towers. But people born under the first sign are passive and nurturing, those born under Testes positive to a fault, while those born under Twin Towers – ruled by Mercury – have a keen business sense. I'd like to have a little of all those qualities, if you can call them that; or rather, I'd like to, but only a little, not too much, just when I needed them.

The woman tries to focus her mind on something more in keeping with the situation. She doesn't quite manage it and returns to the subject.

With my ascendant in Eyes, you'd think I'd be looking and looking all the time, but ever since I arrived I've felt as if there were something obliging me to keep my eyes permanently shut, thus preventing any light from entering my brain; a light that might force me to ask such questions as: what's a girl like me doing in a place like this?

This place is my country – I've returned to my own country – and I'm not exactly a girl any more, on the contrary, but I'm getting sidetracked again, inventing, going off at a tangent, instead of.

That's the way she is and she can't help it.

She went into this country club in search of refuge, so that she could gradually begin to understand, to answer certain sempiternal questions. She went into it the way one goes into hospital, not the way one goes into a wood or the sea or a trance. In search of refuge. Spiritual refuge, as they call it, until some warm breeze fills her sails again and she can once more move on. This dead calm that comes from within troubles her, but what hope is there of moving

2

on for someone who's already travelled halfway round the world?

The woman needs rest. She's returned to her country after a long absence and she finds it hard to fit into this new reality which is so alien, so different from the one she left behind. She lies in bed and perhaps recomposes her thoughts, relives and reconstructs as best she can.

The other day, her friend Carla, well, she's not really a friend, not a very old friend at least, her new friend Carla, found her lying around at home and said:

'You can't stay shut up in here, why don't you go and get some fresh country air? I'll give you the key to my bungalow at the club, well it's just the one room really. Very small but cosy. At least there'll be a few distractions there. If you stay in town you'll roast in this heat and for what? To lie around here half-dead, like a zombie.'

I can't move, she'd protested. How do you expect me to go anywhere? But she'd accepted the offer just to get rid of friend Carla. She packed a bag with the bare essentials: white sheets, a white nightgown and an empty notebook. All very emblematic. And she set off for this unknown but singularly unthreatening destination. Or so she thought then.

Carla had told her: The club isn't one of those flash places, it might not seem much to someone like you coming from abroad, but it's actually very private and exclusive. They don't let just anyone in.

Carla didn't breathe a word about the club's location nor about certain extracurricular activities there and,

3

besides, the woman might well have thought it was nothing to do with her anyway. At this stage of the game, she was still very innocent.

Now that she's actually at the country club, she doesn't want to know anything about anything – yet. Carla had told her that María would take excellent care of her, without actually explaining who María was, and the woman wasn't interested in the who but in the how and that's why she hadn't even spoken to María when she got there, hadn't even introduced herself or asked her for anything. María therefore addresses her as 'Señora' and she enjoys being the 'Señora', lying in bed, with no desire to move.

The place seems very sparsely furnished. When she arrived, she noticed that the curtains were closed and, in that warm half-darkness, she was glad to be able to get into bed as quickly as possible. She pulled the sheet up over her head and pretended she was in a tent in the middle of the desert with the Arab, with a capital A, the one she'd read about as an adolescent, surreptitiously, thinking it was really racy stuff, as they used to say then. She thought about Manucha who'd lent her the book about a thousand years ago, she thought about Beto and Richa and about the others, and felt absolutely no desire to pick up the phone and say Hi, I'm back home, I'm here to stay, long time no see. She didn't feel like saying anything to them. Nothing. Even though the phone is within easy reach, on the bedside table, next to her handbag containing her address book.

Besides, sleep soon got the better of her, that first night.

She's still sleeping now, even though it's daytime; she hasn't realized it because the curtains are drawn. A sleep cure, you might say. Do no noises drift in from outside? What noises there are seem muffled, for the moment.

2

María the maid, however, does come in, more in order
to poke her nose in where it isn't wanted than to offer
her services. An actress playing the part of a maid,
the Señora had said to herself the day she arrived, the
moment she saw María. Maybe it was the big bed in
the middle of that unique setting that made her feel
as if she were standing on a stage. The Señora used
to like acting too, in private, and when she saw the
bed she knew at once the role for her: Sleeping Beauty
in the forest. Something traditional, light. Just what
she needed. There wasn't much else there to distract
her. To the left, the aforementioned heavy curtain,
presumably concealing the French windows that
opened on to the aforesaid forest; to the right,
opposite the curtain, taking up almost the whole wall,

a huge state-of-the-art television screen which she merely gave a bored glance and instantly forgot.

She went to bed and hours and hours went by, possibly days, and she let them go by, dozing off again and again, falling back into a deep sleep and she's still sleeping lightly when María comes in, having knocked in vain, and startles her.

'I'm sorry, Señora,' María says. 'I didn't know you were still asleep, I thought you'd gone to the club-house for breakfast. Or lunch, since it's so late. But you're right to sleep. After all, that's why people come to this club, to rest. To forget all their problems. It's the ideal place for forgetting. Exactly what you need, Señora.'

Why won't she leave me in peace? the Señora wonders, but she knows that now she won't be able to get back to sleep.

'Forgive me if I'm bothering you, Señora.'

She'd like to say that no, she doesn't forgive her, but politeness wins the day and she says:

'You frightened me, María. I was dreaming, I had a nightmare.'

María doesn't like this idea. The country club is unprepared for such subversive activities. The Señora reassures her: it was a very frivolous nightmare, quite funny really. And the marvellous thing was, it was in Spanish. After years of dreaming in English, I'm finally dreaming in Spanish again. And she realizes that, among other things, that's why she's come back, in order not to think or dream in other languages any more. For that reason, out of friendliness and perhaps because she needs to talk to someone, she recounts to the maid what no longer seems such a nightmare.

'It was about prices, a very topical nightmare, very up-to-the-minute, if you like. I was asking: "Why is that appliance so expensive if everything's imported?" And the salesman replied: "Because the gears are oiled with corn oil, locally produced, and you know how the price of foodstuffs has gone up." '

She laughs at her own dream which, now that she's awake, has been wiped clean of everything that had seemed so ominous when she was asleep.

María doesn't find the story funny. María doesn't laugh for just anyone and, besides, she prefers to stick to facts.

'If you don't mind my saying,' she says to the Señora, 'I don't think your dream was much of a nightmare. You've been out of the country for a long time, haven't you? Doña Carla told me that you'd been abroad, that's why you don't know how quickly prices go up here. It's incredible, hyperinflation they call it, we're world champions at that too. Do you know, the photographer in bungalow 7A was sent by a foreign magazine to photograph the prices here, and he simply couldn't, he said, because they came out all blurred. Prices move too quickly for the camera here, you know.'

In other circumstances, the Señora might have found this kind of rather clumsy irony amusing, or else it might have provoked some sociological reflection on her country's situation or whatever. Now it only awakens in her a wave of guilt. Why have I come back, she asks herself, if I can't even be bothered to find out what's going on around me? How long am I going to stay here playing at being an ostrich? And she senses that, although she's sticking her head in the sand in order not to see what's going on, perhaps the sand has things to teach her too: tiny, subtle grains that glitter and dance and shift beneath the surface tension and then, wham, suddenly it's turned into quicksand and she'd be well advised to come up for air.

'María, would you mind bringing me the newspapers?' she asks, as a first step towards slithering back into the world.

María gets angry and tells her that newspapers aren't allowed at the club, because they're very expensive and, besides, they'd disturb the Señora's rest. The things they publish! As if nothing nice ever happened in the country.

'I could tell you about the nice things,' María suggests encouragingly.

A talking newspaper, the Señora says to herself, that's all I need. She wants to be left in peace, she both wants and doesn't want to do a little more rummaging around in her memory, she'd like to want to do a little more rummaging, and above all to find out *why* she wants to rummage and *what* she's looking for in her own mind, as if she were back in her grandmother's attic, not that her grandmother ever had an attic.

María is unrepentant.

'You're quite right to stay in bed really. Although it might be a good idea to get out just for a moment and let me change the sheets. I haven't seen you on the sportsfield yet. Don't you like fresh air? Don't you like sport? Everyone here plays a lot of sport, the healthy life and all that. You should play tennis, the courts here are excellent. I wouldn't advise golf, though, the course is a bit busy, you know. You could go swimming. Or aren't you feeling well? Do you want me to bring you something? An aspirin? They're hard to get hold of now, but with a bit of luck we might find a dealer who could get us a couple. You'll be paying in dollars, I assume.'

No, the Señora shakes her head. No, she won't.

'A pity, you can get anything with dollars.'

Staring into space, the Señora tells her gruffly, between gritted teeth, not to talk to her about dollars, that she's come back in order to immerse herself in her own language, not to go on living in a world that doesn't belong to her. Which is why she goes on to ask María to draw the curtains and open the window. And then you can leave, I'm fine, don't worry about me. Thank you.

María balks at this. The one thing she won't do for the Señora is open the French windows. She wouldn't open them for anything: everything in its place, what the eyes don't see, etc. After all, the Señora's been away and you never know. You never know. The quiet atmosphere of the room should not be shattered by any sudden shaft of light. Or any sudden noise.

A sharp note does penetrate the room however. It sounds like a bugle.

11

'What's that?' asks the Señora, sitting up in bed and pricking up her ears.

'It's probably the angelus,' replies María, in the tone of someone with far more serious matters on her mind.

'The angelus played on a bugle? Don't be ridiculous. Open the window, María. I came to the countryside to breathe some clean air.'

María digs her heels in.

'It's different at the country club. All the air is clean here.'

'Open the window, María.'

'No. Rather than look out of the window, you should be watching TV. I'll put it on.'

12 María has the necessary equipment on her and, not without a certain pride, she produces the remote control from the pocket of her apron and switches on. The huge screen lights up, the Señora is growing furious and the cheery images on the screen do nothing to placate her, on the contrary. The city is one long party, says the commentator, and the images confirm his words. There's a pedestrian precinct as it was in the old days, where people are strolling along as if they were out shopping with every intention of buying something, just like that, or were off to a café to have a cup of coffee they could actually afford; an avenue full of people hurrying along as if they were on their way to work, as if they had jobs to go to; a vast square in all its leisurely, arboreal splendour.

For a moment, the Señora forgets her anger and is taken in. Perhaps she's right, she says to herself, per-

haps I am missing out, shut away here in the countryside, as it were. I should move, go outside, see what's
going on around me. They tell me the city's changed
a lot; I've heard other things, too, but who knows?
Perhaps the city is one long party and I'm missing out
on it.

'María, open the window,' she says again, as a first
step towards clearing the way for action.

'The programmes are lovely, Señora, now that
they've privatized all the channels. But if you find
them boring, you being used to other things, you
could rent a video recorder. I'll get you one. If you pay
cash, you get twenty per cent off plus tickets for a
raffle. I'll keep the raffle tickets, if you don't mind.'

Suddenly, the Señora doesn't know if she feels suffo-
cated by the maid's chatter or because she needs to
make some contact with the outside world. She won't
be defeated, she won't just lie back in bed, she pulls
herself up a little more and demands that María switch
off the television once and for all. And don't forget
the window, she reminds her. María resists.

'You're the one who gives the orders and I'm supposed to carry them out. But don't forget, you'll soon
be gone but I have to stay here, and my real boss is
Señora Carla and she loves watching television. And
she never opens the French windows. They're never
opened.'

Surreptitiously, with her hand inside her pocket, she
uses the remote control to turn the volume up on the
television. Music has a soothing effect, she thinks.

She's quite wrong. The Señora merely finds the

13

music irritating. The camera, which is now swooping into luxurious cafés, anachronistic and distant, only increases her sense of oppression. She makes as if to get up. María is alarmed.

'Don't get up, it's bad for you. You're ill.'

'I'm not ill. Switch it off.'

'If Dr Bermúdez was here, I'd call him,' wails María. 'But there's something fishy about the new doctor, Dr Alfredi. I don't know how he managed to get into the club. And to think that they blackballed Dr Bermúdez just because his wife got too fat! Now there's this other doctor here, though God knows who recommended him. Do you know, he's got a day job as a taxi driver, to balance the books, he says.'

14   'I don't need a doctor.'

'You've come to live in this country. My country. Our country. I was told that before, you lived in New York: you *must* be ill. A big city, New York, so they say. I wouldn't like it, it's too violent. They're always showing it on the TV. Here, though, things are different, orderly. Just look, isn't that pretty?'

The Señora is beginning to realize that a lot of people are going to think she's mad coming back just now, but she'll be madder still if she has to put up with this chatter for much longer and all these images of a kind of apocalypse in reverse, all the more intimidating because they're false. Are they false? They're probably real, there they are wiping out all the things she doesn't want to see but should see. But it's all too sudden, how can she bear it?

Is my city like that? Is it the way they show

it? Driving in from the airport, I remember cracked pavements, rather less radiant, less well-fed faces . . .

'Now New York really is a violent place,' María insists. 'And you lived there for ten years; there must be a reason for that. What's more they say it's full of beggars, of homeless people sleeping on the main streets. Awful.'

María has turned down the volume on the television in order to be heard and the Señora, who has heard her, is reflecting, a little calmer now, or rather, more resigned, which is not the same thing. She reflects, wonders, and is happy that she's beginning to wonder about things, that the mechanism is slowly grinding into action. She wonders if she is, after all, slightly ill, just a little bit, if she has some symptom that justifies both her need to return and her simultaneous desire not to be here, not to know.

'Perhaps it would be a good idea to call the doctor after all.'

'You're very pale, you know. I can bring Don Gervasio and he can give you a pick-me-up. He knows a lot about herbs and he's a great healer.'

She's stumbled into a madhouse; if she had the strength she'd grab her bags and go back to the city. How lovely it used to be to feel strong, the Señora recalls. She needs to recover from the journey, she thinks, from the jet-lag. It isn't easy coming back after ten years away.

María would like to help the Señora in her re-encounter with reality, if one can put it like that. She turns up the volume on the TV. There you are, Señora, she says. As if it were a gift.

'Leave me to think in peace!' the Señora almost screams and feels that her voice may have come out a little too vehemently.

'Thinking isn't healthy,' María says reproachfully. 'What you need to do, if you don't mind my saying so, is to find some distraction. You've spent two days in bed, if I'm not mistaken. You changed your dollars at the reception desk when you arrived and you still haven't spent a cent. If you don't mind my saying so. If I'm not mistaken. These are not the actions of a well woman. You're in a terrible state, you haven't even got any food in. Look, there's nothing in the fridge, or almost nothing, honestly, you'll be the death of me. What can I say? I'm only pointing it out for your own good. That money has to be spent quickly before it devalues.'

Sometimes you buy silence, sometimes solitude, sometimes you have to use subterfuge to buy the moment of quiet which is all you want. If a steak comes wrapped in a bit of peace and quiet, if coffee comes wrapped in peace and quiet, however ironic it may seem, then fine.

'Here, María, go and do my shopping for me, buy whatever food you think I need,' sighs the besieged Señora.

And she takes out a large, crisp note from her handbag on the bedside table, rustling it temptingly at María. María snatches it up and the Señora seizes the moment:

'And draw the curtains!' she cries. 'That's an order.' She wants it to sound like an order and can't understand why such a simple request should need to become an order. She's almost about to apologize, she didn't come here to boss anyone around, but she feels as if she were gasping for air.

'Draw the curtains, I'm suffocating. Call the doctor.'

María embellishes the order, embroiders upon it, by first switching off the television with her remote control and then going over to the window:

'I'm not only going to draw the curtains, I'm also going to open the French windows. I've got the key. There you are, you asked for it.'

And before the Señora can demand anything else, María picks up her broom and scurries out, shutting the door to the room behind her.

'The doctor!' shouts the Señora, but it's too late. The maid has gone.

3

The gentle evening breeze enters through the now half-open French windows, perhaps lulling the Señora to sleep. Other imponderables enter too, but these the Señora either doesn't notice or doesn't want to notice. She doesn't want to notice. Stretched out on her big white bed in the middle of the room, she's in no mood for such surprises. She appears to be asleep or deep in thought or perhaps immersed in the ancient discipline of transcendental meditation, so fashionable in recent years.

That's why she doesn't notice the manoeuvres taking place outside the window: mere shadows but no less disquieting for that.

Those are military manoeuvres that can be heard outside the window. Military manoeuvres at a country club? Absolutely. However illogical they may seem, the things that happen here can be explained. The Señora hasn't yet realized that her friend Carla's place, called a bungalow in this part of the world, is right on the edge of the country club, barely yards away from what might be designated the frontier. Curled up, facing the television screen and with her back to the window, the Señora sleeps on unaware that the club's manicured lawns come headlong up against the vast, ugly chain-link fence, a human chicken coop, which, together with a few scrawny, dried-up bushes, is intended to separate her from a wasteland on which the only thing that grows are houses made out of cardboard and tin.

20   A few shots ring out. On this side of the fence the military gentlemen are practising their shooting, taking aim at cutout figures, apparently doing their weapons training. Should the Señora be warned? Should she be woken, alerted? What should one do in such cases? Doubt creeps in through the half-open French windows along with another shadow growing gradually more substantial. It isn't a jaguar on the prowl or some kind of fabulous beast; it would seem to be – and indeed it is – a young soldier in fatigues dragging himself forward on his elbows, his belly to the ground. He advances with great difficulty, puffing and panting, but he keeps going and, that's why, to keep up his courage, he mutters to himself as he goes, huff, puff, in between gulps of air.

'I've just, turned, eighteen, my father says, "be a man", my mother says, "don't listen, to, your father", my little sister, Patri, says, "come and, play with me", my best, friend, says, well, it doesn't matter, what he says. The family's, the most, important, thing, in life. Juanjo is, my best friend. I'm, Lucho. They call me, Lucho, my real name's, José Luis, but they, call me, Lucho. They call me, other things, too. They called me, up, for military service. AND HERE I AM. Be a man, my father says.'

If only the Señora knew, if she could see how close he is, approaching the bed, slowly sliding in among the lace ruffles on the valance, slipping under the bed, her high brass bed. If only she knew what her bed knows and what it is now, apparently, swallowing whole. Devouring the conscript.

Time follows a different rhythm inside this room, **21** time has stopped and bears no relation whatsoever to the feverish activity of the shadows outside. The shadows crawl on their bellies, squat down. These upheavals have no place in the Señora's peaceful sleep, in her somnolent state. At least not yet.

4

Only María can rouse her from her state of bliss. She may have knocked, but whether she did or not, she certainly didn't bother to wait for the still sleeping Señora to say 'Come in'. She arrives laden down with packages and, sure that this time she'll be well received, she doesn't bother to enter quietly, on the contrary. The Señora opens her eyes, sits up in bed, and is about to say something, doubtless some word of protest, she's always protesting, this Señora, but María gets in before her:

'Look at all I've brought you, Señora. You won't be able to complain of hunger now.'

Hunger, thinks the Señora, hunger. I've heard that word a lot lately. In my day it wasn't much used in this part of the world.

María has no time for unspoken thoughts. With enormous pride she places the packages on the bed around the Señora, like Christmas presents around a Christmas tree (except Christmas trees don't complain).

'Flour, sugar, eggs, ham, cheese, rice, beans, lentils,' says the maid, listing her purchases.

It's a fine display. The Señora has just thought of the comparison with Christmas and the idea seems to please her. She says proudly:

'This country's the breadbasket of the world.'

'It was, Señora, a long time ago, things are different now. Just look at this: Italian spaghetti, tinned tomatoes in their juice from Chile, Brazilian palmhearts and Spanish sardines.'

Things have gone too far, beyond a joke. The Señora is alarmed. How long do you think I'm going to stay here? she asks María. I don't need all this food, there's enough here to feed an army.

'You gave me the money and I invested it for you. They're all imperishable goods.'

'And what about the change? You must have some change for me.'

María looks at her as if she were a Martian. She must be a Martian, where has she been? And purely out of deference to Señora Carla, who understands everything so well, she deigns to explain to the alien.

'Your change will be no good to you tomorrow. As soon as you get some money in your hand, you have to spend it at once, otherwise it devalues.'

She takes a tin of palmhearts, a can of olive oil and

a kilo of sugar. By way of a tip, she says, everyone does it, she says. If you knew how difficult it is to get sugar . . .

There are so many things she should know. She's only just beginning to get an inkling, to glimpse out of the corner of her eye what is going on beyond those deceiving French windows, which do not show what lies on the other side but, rather, stand open in such a way as to reflect the distant apparently tree-filled landscape to either side and a green, green field that bears no relation to the desolate field beyond the chain-link fence.

Perhaps the reflections stop me seeing something I should see but don't want to, or something that doesn't want to be seen but which I sense is there; perhaps if the French windows were opened wide I would be able at last to enter that reality, but what is reality? What am I talking about here in this bed piled high with provisions. Food to keep my mouth shut? A case of why complain, when the cupboard's full?

María needs to catch her eye again.

'I'll turn the television on, the programmes are excellent at this time of day.'

'No.'

'You don't appreciate how hard I've worked for you. If you'd seen what the supermarket was like! Full. Packed. Everyone wants to buy before the prices go up again. You've no idea the trouble I had getting a trolley.'

The Señora is no longer listening to her. She thinks: if I yawn, she'll leave, she must at least respect my need for rest. One yawn brings another in its train. If I yawn, I start to feel tired and presumably I must be, for now anyway, until I get acclimatized.

'You're tired, I'll leave you, it's late,' says María, perhaps taking pity on her or perhaps lulling her into sleep, so that she will go to sleep again and go on sleeping, since she doesn't play tennis and because, far off, the powerful floodlights are being switched on above the courts and the military manoeuvres are no longer shadows, you can see them clear as day through the French windows which, with the light shining through them from outside, have lost their mirror-like quality. They're changing the guard, María watches out of the corner of her eye, while she arranges the Señora's packages neatly on the bed and tucks her in or, rather, smooths the quilt a little, as well as she can without disturbing the pile of food. She talks to her quietly and the Señora whispers: To think that . . . and María interrupts her: Don't think. She says it softly, in a very low voice. Thinking's bad for you, don't think, she repeats, and when the Señora has closed her eyes tight shut María imitates the marching troops outside the window and goosesteps over to the door.

26

5

This bed is sailing through smooth-skinned, treacherous waters. Occasionally the bed trembles and the Señora thinks that sleep or memory or some untimely recollection or twinge of conscience are playing tricks on her. But it's not that. She thinks she's caught glimpses of soldiers reflected in the window panes and now she feels something like a gentle jolting lulling her to sleep, though why she doesn't know. She feels lighter. She feels as if the bed was lighter.

She pretended to be asleep to get rid of María and she thinks of all the other times she's pretended to be asleep for one reason or another. Should she wake up? Wake up properly? Her conscience . . .

Something interrupts her thoughts. She suddenly sees a hand appear from underneath the bed and the hand, with infinite care and delicacy, very slowly steals a package of food. Another hand appears immediately afterwards, and another, each one swifter than the last, each one relieving her of another package.

A few peals of laughter ring out beneath the bed, which does not tremble now, though it might as well, for it feels to her as if it does and a shudder runs through her at the sight of those multiplying hands.

'What do you want?' shouts the Señora. And the hands respond by coming out from underneath the bed.

'No, wait,' she manages to murmur, shaking off her surprise, setting aside her fear.

The hands obey for a moment, hang there motion-less and then quickly resume their task.

'Take whatever you need but be careful, don't break anything,' says the Señora, almost sighing.

The hands attempt haphazard caresses, fingers like feathers brush her skin, grateful, and she joins in the game.

'And don't break me either . . .'

But everything is quiet now, the bed smooth, as if nothing had ever been there, not even a tiny stock cube.

She's quick to recover from surprises, quick to see the positive side of things. Is this what I came back for? she asks herself. To be stripped of everything and have to start again? Or to fulfil the dream of having a bed of my own? At least they didn't take the bed.

'Oh well,' she says in a loud voice. 'I never do any cooking anyway.'

And she's just about to look under the bed to unveil the mystery, with that old, fearful childhood feeling of wanting and not wanting to look. I never do any cooking anyway, so don't worry, she says again, to placate possible monsters, again as she had when she was a child, except that now it's not for her to decide, others will decide for her and then when she's finally screwed up enough courage and is about to lean over the side of the bed, a cloud of white smoke chokes her. It's tear gas, she recognizes it from her student days, she coughs, weeps and almost misses the glint of fixed bayonets appearing from beneath the bed. But she hears the blows.

She cries out.

A single short, irrepressible cry.

'Maríííа!'

María responds instantly, too instantly, as if she'd been lurking outside the door or perhaps just waiting there.

'Do you need me, Señora?'

'There are people here. I mean, soldiers. Where are we?'

And María, as if she were addressing a halfwit or some poor idiot who knows nothing of the world (and in that she may be right), explains that, yes, she's delighted to say that there are soldiers, this is one of the most privileged of country clubs, one of the most select, most frequented and best protected.

'Not that well protected, they made off with everything.'

'Who did?'

The Señora doesn't know, she shakes her head, she can't find words now to express that strangeness, that sense of dislocation. I don't know, she murmurs, and then adds: underneath the bed. She points, cautiously, not putting her hand too near for fear of getting bitten.

'Underneath the bed?' repeats María, making the Señora all too conscious of how foolish that sounds. 'There's nothing underneath the bed. I do the cleaning myself and I know that there's nothing under the bed, not even a bit of fluff. I clean very thoroughly, Señora, you can be sure of that. Now let me just change the sheets. Because of the crumbs, I mean.'

Naturally the Señora asks what crumbs she's talking about and María has no wish to treat the Señora like a madwoman, but if she's been playing around with the food that María herself brought her, if she's eaten it all already . . .

'If there are soldiers around here, I'm going to have to go,' says the Señora, interrupting her, still harping on the same theme.

For some reason, her proposal seems to alarm María. After all, Señora Carla did phone her and ask her to take good care of this lady, so she can't just let her leave like that, all disgruntled, who knows what she'll go telling people if she leaves in a bad mood, spending all that money on food and now this, it would be best to placate her, persuade her. This is the best place in the best country in the world, a very special place, like she said; Señora Carla said I should take extra care of this woman because she needs to rest, though God knows why, she doesn't look ill.

'Don't leave, Señora, at least not so suddenly. You'll come to appreciate how lucky you are to be here. Don't get so upset, you think too much.'

'Too much! You can never think too much. Bring me some tea, María, that's all I ask.'

'Just as well you don't want coffee, with the price it is today. Besides coffee would make you jumpy.'

'I didn't say anything about coffee.'

'And I wouldn't have brought you any either. Life here should be leisurely, "easy-going" as they say in the club brochure. Not like life on the other side of the fence, it's terrible there. The country's on the other side. Or what they call reality. But you've nothing to worry about here, Señora, everything's taken care of. All neat and orderly.'

6

As if he were in a different scene – not that anyone is
watching him – the little soldier, Lucho, has emerged
from his refuge under the bed. He looks more dishev-
elled, one or two buttons on his shirt are undone, but
he doesn't care because no one – I repeat no one – is
watching him. Despite that, he still doesn't stand up,
preferring to crawl along as he did before. While
María tries to persuade the Señora to stay, he's search-
ing for something on the floor, dragging himself for-
wards on his elbows in his best trench-warfare style.
He rapidly finds what he's looking for: a small tin of
pâté that had apparently rolled out of reach during
the plundering of the bed. He picks it up in his mouth,
like an obedient dog, and so this time, having his
mouth full, he doesn't mumble to himself as he goes,

but executes an about turn quick march, in other
words, he crawls back to the bed and slides under it
again, disappearing among the ruffles.

María, meanwhile, is still doing her best to convince
the Señora of the delights of the club:

'Oh yes, this is a lovely place, immaculately kept.
It's a shame the soldiers killed off the hedge trying
out their defoliants. But they do marvels with the new
equipment. "New weapons for a new type of soldier",
that's what they say. Of course, now that they've killed
off the hedge with the defoliants, you can see over to
the other side of the fence. Not a pretty sight, I know.
That's why, you see, in the bungalows on the north
side, we always leave the curtains closed. A purely
aesthetic measure, as Señora Carla says, and she knows
a lot about such things.'

'I don't care. If there are soldiers here I'm leaving.'

'Everyone wants to leave the country.'

'It's the club I'm leaving.'

'It comes to the same thing.'

The maid rambles on so that the Señora begins to
lose interest, to lose her resolve. It is night and the
soldiers seem to have been summoned to rest or to
some other urgent and equally unobtrusive duty. They
seem aware that, since they're not in a traditional
location, they must not overdo their manoeuvres. Not
that they relax the discipline. Or the security measures. A spotlight constantly sweeps the area on the
other side of the chain-link fence, where what before
was a bare field full of shacks is now a heaving mass
of humanity. The soldiers can do nothing, the shanty

town is out of their jurisdiction, but they doubtless watch with growing disquiet the progress of what would seem to be the cooking of a communal stew.

That's exactly what it is. Someone contributes a packet of rice, another noodles, a few tins of vegetables, stock cubes. Everyone has something to add to the vast, boiling vat and, though contented, they do their best to remain calm, as if afraid that the people on the other side of the fence might invade and eat their food. One young girl moves away from the group, which is now gathering with tins and bowls to empty the vat and fill their bellies. Patricia, Patri, someone calls to her, but the imprudent girl goes over to the barbed-wire fence and in turn calls, slightly anxiously. Lucho, she calls, Lucho, come and play with me. The others have all gone off to eat, ravenously, happily.

Defoliants or no, María has always behaved as if the hedge were still in place and has never wanted to know about the vicissitudes of life beyond the boundaries of the club. That's why she talks on, positioning herself between the Señora and the pathetic scene outside.

'There *are* some soldiers here, but they act as a kind of guarantee. And we're glad of it. They're all young officers, our country's finest. It's exciting having them here among us; they're training the commando groups. The bravest and most valiant of soldiers.'

And to dispel any lingering doubts about the truth of what she says, she plunges her hand into the deep pocket of her apron and brings out a much-read copy of a booklet issued by the American army. This is the

Manual, she explains to the Señora in a tone of deep respect. This is something we do admire about the Yanks. You've just come from there, you're bound to know it. *The Challenge of Combat Weapons*, it's called. Look, look what it says here, I haven't got my glasses with me, but I know it by heart, listen: 'The qualities needed to win a place in the Special Forces are resourcefulness and stamina.' Isn't that beautiful? These are *our* country's special forces, and here we are, privileged women, as the soldiers tell us, enjoying a place among them that we didn't even have to fight for.

'I want to leave,' is all the Señora can say, though she's still quite unable to move.

36   'They're the glory of our nation, Señora. And proud of it. Look what else it says: "You have the best weaponry and the best training. With us you will face the greatest of life's challenges: yourself!" Here, you have it, Señora, read it.'

And with a gesture of Olympian grandeur, of unparalleled generosity, she tosses the treasured booklet onto the bed. The Manual. Go on, read it, she insists, it'll make you feel better.

7

María has finally withdrawn, again, and one presumes that she won't be back, it's late now, time to go to sleep, perhaps, although, the Señora thinks, she really must pay more attention to what's going on around her, try to understand, if understanding were not too much to hope for in this country and in these unfortunate times.

The Señora's thoughts are no longer occupied by spurious horoscopes, she's thinking that she should be thinking and yet she can't, she fears that, on some subliminal level, she may be obeying María's order: don't think, thinking's bad for you, it upsets you. She's not upset, just tired, tired. Perhaps she should, after all, ask for Don Gervasio and his restorative. Or the doctor who doubles as a taxi driver, he must be an interesting sort, lively, with lots of stories to tell, just what she needs. Is it? Anyway, in complete contravention of her inexplicable law of passivity, she picks up the phone and asks the operator to send the doctor. Afterwards she feels drained, with barely enough strength to replace the receiver.

The military give no thought to her. She's just a poor wretched woman lying in bed, having brought with her from her time abroad who knows what infectious diseases. The disease of indifference, for a start, which prevents her seeing the brilliant national destiny of which they are the embodiment, the personification. And so, because this woman is just some left-wing nobody and because she's undoubtedly asleep, they have no hesitation in surrounding her territory.

The aide-de-camp is first through the French windows and he doesn't even glance at the bed. He brings with him a small folding table and places it on one side of the vast room, near the chest of drawers. Then he brings in a folding chair which he places near the table, its back to the Señora. The location has been carefully thought out; they've obviously been doing this throughout the time the bungalow has been unoccupied.

With a step that manages to be both martial and elastic, thanks to a combination of natural vigour and the fine quality of his boots, Major Vento enters the room and sits down at the table. He snaps his fingers and the ADC reappears, this time with a tray bearing a bottle of champagne, one of those tall glasses known as flute-glasses, which the Major carefully examines, proud that he knows the name, and a mug filled with a red, viscous liquid.

The Major questions his ADC as the latter places the mug on the table. Where's that new conscript got to? he asks.

'I don't know, sir, he's a most undisciplined young fellow.'

'Riffraff!' exclaims the Major indignantly, as he struggles with the champagne cork, which, for a moment, looks as if it's going to get the better of him. 'They're not like us, I don't know how they even manage to get into the club . . . I mean the regiment. Find him for me. I want him here, now.'

And, having finally triumphed over the cork, which proceeds to do its festive imitation of a cannon shot, he adds:

'Have him present himself here face down, crawling on his elbows. Those are his marching orders for today.'

The Señora, meanwhile, has picked up the Manual that María left behind and, not without a certain distaste, re-reads the words: 'You have the best weaponry and the best training. With us you will face the greatest of life's challenges: yourself.'

Galvanized not by the Major's order but by the cannon shot of the champagne cork, Lucho peers out from under the bed, from among the lace ruffles, and crawls resignedly towards his superior officer.

'Be a man, my father said,' he mumbles, but the Major remains unmoved by this pathetic show of filial devotion. He's on the point of giving him a kick with his fine leather boots, which seem tailor-made for the purpose. Lucho, seeing them at close quarters, jumps to his feet and stands to attention.

'Sorry, sir. I say things I don't really think and think things I can't say.'

'Don't think! Say everything! EVERYTHING. Nothing must be kept secret from the army. From the Fatherland.'

An ominous silence falls but Lucho doesn't hear it. Instead he hears Patri calling to him again, from the shanty town.

'My sister's calling me,' he says at last.

As we have seen, the Major has no interest in family matters. He says indignantly:

40   'You're a soldier at the service of the Nation. You have no sister and you have only one mother, your Country! Don't be insolent, soldier. Down on the floor!'

Lucho responds at once and lies face down on the floor, and the Señora, who's now watching the scene, is filled with pity. Pity for the poor conscript and even more for herself, the woman who sought refuge in a bed and now finds herself completely adrift. Adrift with the army, to make matters worse.

'Though it may not look like it, this is a barracks and we are crack troops,' Major Vento tells the conscript, not for the first time. 'Squat!' he orders, at the same time filling his glass. 'You are privileged to be amongst us,' he explains to the conscript between sips. 'We are the toughest, the best-trained, the fastest. Face down on the ground! Forward, march!'

And proud of his ingenuity, he points to the bed and says: 'Run, soldier! Faster. Run. Jump that obstacle.'

The Señora sees him coming towards her and, although she can't believe what's happening, she manages to duck under the quilt, turning herself into a white mound for the soldier to fly over, as ordered. He leaps the bed once, twice, then luckily the order changes. 'Squat!' the Major shouts again, saving the Señora the probable embarrassment, the consequent shock and the inevitable thump of a conscript landing on her soft human form. A quilt is not much of a buffer.

Major Vento issues orders and counterorders at the speed of light. The space is too small for such manoeuvres, but what they lack in breadth, they make up for in complexity. Now touch Christ's balls! howls the Major and the Señora can't resist peering languidly out from beneath the sheets. She sees the soldier jumping into the air, his arms upstretched, higher, higher, shouts the Major. Christ's balls! . . . The things you learn in bed, the Señora says to herself.

No one seems in the least concerned about her and she begins to find the whole thing interesting. She watches, only her eyelashes showing above the bedclothes and, as she watches, it occurs to her that what she sees compromises her and so she closes her eyes tight shut, but the act of closing her eyes, trying to ignore the unignorable, what is happening under her very nose, at her bedside you might say, is like erecting a very thin screen that protects her from nothing. On the contrary. It's better to watch and be able to see

41

where the next blow is coming from: the next leap. She's still frightened though and withdraws her head – like a tortoise into a shell of soft, white lace – then sticks it out again because she can't believe what's going on, thinks perhaps it's a nightmare, a bad dream that's mildly funny but otherwise disturbing, better to follow the flow of the dream and watch to see if it changes into a merry-go-round or a walk along the beach.

And to think that she got into this bed in order to rest, to piece things together. The orders continue to thunder forth and the soldier obeys: down on your elbows, up, run, down on the ground, run, up, down on the ground, up, jump, ru . . .

Until he reaches the feet of the Major sitting on his folding chair in front of his folding table and his bottle of champagne. The Señora sees it and sees that it's no dream, although the Major seems to consider *her* a dream, or even less than a dream, a nonentity, a despicable speck of dirt. The Señora sees everything and she gasps along with the conscript. Ahh, she says with him, and luckily no one pays any attention to her, ahh, she says involuntarily, and suddenly disappears beneath the sheets: I wasn't here, I didn't say anything, I didn't see anything, I don't know anything. At least that last statement is true.

Her disgust is quite justified. The Major has offered the soldier the mug and its viscous contents. He's raised it up like a chalice or as if proposing a toast and ordered:

'Drink!'

And poor Lucho, a conscript only by constitutional decree and because he just happens to have reached the tender age of consent, has taken only one sip and spat it out again, almost retching, leaving a repellent stain on the pale carpet.

'Bull's blood, soldier, that's the drink for victors,' Major Vento tells him in his most thunderous martial voice.

And he adds:

'You have not drunk from the cup of glory. You are not made for victory. A failure to obey orders, soldier. You're under arrest.'

In response to an imperceptible gesture from the Major, the ADC comes back into the room and calls in a couple of soldiers who quickly overpower Lucho. They're about to take him away, but the tirade is not yet over:

'Consider this a great honour, soldier. We all are or will be prisoners at some time in our lives, in order to discipline the body and the mind. To know the harsh side of life, to make us even harder.'

From the inside pocket of his jacket he takes out a copy of the by now famous Manual, the booklet issued by the American armed forces, a bit like the Bible, and waves it in front of the prisoner's eyes.

'If you can prove your courage here, you can prove it anywhere. Then you can look over your shoulder and shout the proud slogan of the marines that has echoed down the years: "Follow me!" ' he declaims fervently, with no need to refer to the text.

The Señora tries to remember the quote, sensing

that doing so might be useful to her some day. She tries to remember both the quote and the scene she has witnessed and to add it to some other elusive memory. She fails. All that's left, beating in a small corner of her brain, are the final words uttered by the Major and she knows that they weren't meant for her, that she can't follow, that she must stay there, not moving, not being, not following anyone, just stay there and, perhaps, with a great deal of luck, remember.

44

8

The spotlights have been switched off, it's almost eleven o'clock at night and at the country club everything is dark and still, as if nothing were happening there. But something is, and in the still air, accompanied only by the sweet murmur of the casuarina trees – like the murmuring of a far distant sea – comes the sound of voices, clear as a bell, unmistakable. The sound reaches the bungalow, where the Señora is trying at last to get to sleep.

'No, not naked! No!' she hears and she recognizes, as anyone would, the terrified voice of the conscript, so young, and shrill with fear.

'Yes,' says the much deeper voice of the Major. 'Yes, naked as the naked truth. Naked as the naked Fatherland before the oppressor. Naked as the earth, bare for lack of seeds. You must learn to be what you are, soldier. A pathetic heap of naked rubbish. You must be reborn: you will no longer be the unfortunate wretch you were, not just another poor immigrant from the interior, on the other side of the fence. You are now a member of a crack regiment and you must learn to deserve our glorious uniform.'

The Señora doesn't want to hear any more, she doesn't want this brutish reality to touch her. She covers her ears. This is too much, she thinks, tomorrow I'll leave, if I can, if I can get myself together, if I can leave this bed, if I can get beyond the stupid chamber pot that idiot María has forgotten to empty. Tomorrow I'll leave, if I can. If they let me.

And she thinks this ignorant of the fact that the conscript, naked now, has been handcuffed, gagged and placed in a pit just big enough for a man to stand up in, a man of a slightly larger build than the conscript but not much. The sappers dug the pit specifically for that purpose, because there'll always be at least one prisoner: it's all part of the drill, part of the training they undergo, these commandos, who want not only to be the best but also the toughest, the most seasoned, the best prepared for a life of combat.

No one knows what the club authorities make of these excavations bang in the middle of the golf course, but they seem to have resigned themselves to it, if, that is, they're at liberty to say what they think, to express an opinion.

The hole in the ground has a heavy metal cover, on which the soldiers have been ordered to place a cassette player, of doubtful origin, taken from a car perhaps, but which from this moment on will deafen the prisoner with Cuban music.

'Come on then, move it! You'd better keep dancing, if you don't want to freeze to death tonight. Now you'll find out who the real enemy is and how far we're prepared to go to break you,' they yell at the prisoner.

And then nothing, only the music.

The wind seems to have blown the French windows shut, but the Señora would like someone to draw the curtains too, to isolate her, protect her, cut her off. How can she think that, when she believed herself so brave, living all that time abroad and in such difficult circumstances? And now this: turn out the light so that they don't see her, hide underneath the blankets.

9

The club clock strikes eleven. At night. The hour of forgetting. Don't think, María had told her, thinking's bad for you, and she tries to obey her. She almost misses María.

That's why she says 'Come in' with such urgency when, shortly afterwards, the doorbell rings. Come in, she says, as she switches on the light again.

But at the door stands not María but a stranger. I'm Dr Alfredi, says the man, to reassure her. You asked to see a doctor, he explains, just in case, because the woman in the bed is looking at him in alarm and that's hardly surprising: he's still wearing his taxi driver clothes – blue check shirt and a cap worn at a jaunty angle.

Seeing his future patient's surprise, the so-called Dr

Alfredi hurriedly removes the cap and the shirt and places them on a chair. He's brought his doctor's gown with him and, in something of a rush, he puts it on and takes his stethoscope out of the pocket.

'Right,' he says.

She seems rather less alarmed now. He walks over to her, a kindly look on his face. He's young, athletic, well-built, a fact that does not escape the Señora's notice. His easy stride and his smile inspire confidence.

She returns his smile, from the bed, which is, after all, the best place to receive a doctor.

'Now what seems to be the matter? Where can I take you . . . I mean, what's troubling you?'

'I don't know that anything much is troubling me . . . I don't really know why I asked them to call you, it was an impulse. In fact I was fine until this evening, though now I think I may be running a fever. It must be the shock, I suppose. The situation here is so strange, so different. I know it isn't easy coming back to a country after ten years away, but I wasn't expecting it to be like this.'

The doctor seems interested as, with extreme delicacy, he places the stethoscope on her throat.

'Coming back?'

'Yes. I left during the dictatorship and I've just returned, imagining it would be different somehow. But I must have some kind of infection, I even see soldiers on my bed.'

The doctor moves the stethoscope gently along her

collar bone, but he's listening more attentively to her words than to her heart or lungs.

'On your bed?' he asks and there's a suggestive undertone to his voice.

She responds with a dispassionate account of events. Yes, on the bed and underneath, I see them everywhere. Soldiers, ugh!

He then clears up a few of her doubts and patiently explains that it's not that unusual here, given that the military have set up a training camp on the golf course.

'They're on manoeuvres because they say the barracks isn't safe any more, they say the timber in the stockade is rotten. In the club, though, everything's perfectly well organized, orderly, so they say. What are you worried about?'

'I just find it very disturbing.'

'That depends on how you look at it. There's a positive side to it too. They usually do their manoeuvres during the day, and by day I'm a cabbie and I like to think things are under control, well regimented. When I'm a taxi driver I like order.'

'And when you're a doctor?'

'When I'm a doctor I don't know. The human organism, apparently so orderly, is ruled by very idiosyncratic and not always predictable laws. May I?'

And he gently slips off the strap of her white nightgown in order to immerse himself a little more deeply in his search for the body's not always predictable laws and murmurings. You may, she says.

'You're all alone here, are you?'

'I'm on my own, yes.'

51

'And what's a pretty woman like you doing sleeping in a single solitary bed?'

'What a stupid question, Doctor, how very unprofessional of you. It's because I can't sleep in two beds at once. Because for the moment I find one bed quite sufficient. And because I can't move.'

'You can't?'

She tries to explain to him that physically she can move, she doesn't need drugs or anything like that, perhaps just some sort of tranquillizer, something to help her sleep and not have nightmares now that she finds herself in the midst of all this unexpected turmoil.

'Turmoil?'

52

'That's what I said. Perhaps that's why I can't move, but I'm not paralysed, I haven't got cramp, I'm not exhausted or quadriplegic or catatonic or autistic or run down or weak or liverish or anything. It's morally that I can't move. I have no will. I've completely lost my will power. I'd like to get up but I can't. I let myself be bossed around by the maid, I let those soldiers, who have nothing whatsoever to do with me, invade my privacy. Well, almost. I'd like to leave and I can't, I mean it.'

The doctor wants to know if she can't or if she simply doesn't want to.

'I *can't.*'

He tells her not to worry, he'll see what he can do to help. He advises her, though, that his diagnosis of her illness would be that it was 'benign but persistent'.

'You're suffering from what we call "willow sickness", it's very common in this part of the world. Sufferers show no desire to move, only to look, to remember, to tie up loose ends.'

'Mustn't overdo it, though, doctor. I'm a prudent woman and I know that remembering can be unhealthy.'

'Not at all.'

But someone had told her so a little while ago, they'd told her it was better not to think or remember. They'd said it almost like a threat and now she can't even remember who it was. It's obviously easily learnt this forgetting.

'At the moment I feel as if someone was trying to wipe my memory clean, I don't know, obliterate it with new inscriptions. I don't understand it at all.'

'That happens a lot here. What else is worrying you?'

The woman tells him her dream about prices, of her fear on the one hand and of her happiness to be dreaming in Spanish again on the other.

'Such conflicts are typical of any period of readaptation,' the doctor-cum-taxi driver says to console her and she allows herself to be consoled, thinking that he must presumably be something of a philosopher too.

The doctor is good at that, at consoling people: he has the best possible remedy and, nonchalantly, he shifts the stethoscope to her forehead, her eyelids, her lips. He does so delicately, as if he were touching her with his fingers and in fact the stethoscope is now

53

pleasantly warm from its prolonged contact with the Señora's body.

You shouldn't worry so much, the doctor advises, although that isn't the kind of advice she wants. She doesn't know what she wants. That's why he warns her to listen to what her body is telling her.

'As I think I mentioned before, the body is governed by very idiosyncratic rules.'

It's clear that *he* has listened to her body, through the stethoscope that is. He's sitting on the bed now and keeps moving a little closer. He starts sounding her chest, tapping the back of his hand with the tips of his fingers.

'*Very* idiosyncratic,' agrees the woman, just to say something.

'There's the pleasure principle.'

Of course.

'And the principle of letting yourself be heard, of just lying around, and . . . Does it hurt you here?'

'No, not at all.'

'Or here?'

It obviously doesn't hurt her there, or anywhere else for that matter.

The person who is hurting, everywhere, is the poor imprisoned conscript, Lucho, stuck down a tiny, damp hole. No one bothers with him now, only another young soldier, who's been left on duty there, on guard duty, a few feet from the Señora's French windows, with his back to a scene that might otherwise distract him, obedient though he is, perhaps almost a little proud of his mission, determined not to go to sleep, not to be taken by surprise, not to catch cold.

Very few people would feel afraid of catching cold with a doctor by their side. The Señora is not one of them and so she allows the doctor gradually to undress her, not necessarily in order to undergo a clinical examination either.

The diseases of the memory cannot usually be detected using ultrasound or be cured with potions. Willow sickness, that well-known local disease diagnosed by Dr Alfredi, who is with us here today, would seem to require a more immediate therapy, personal and affectionate. At least in this particular and unusually attractive case. Which is why Dr Alfredi has also got undressed and is eagerly preparing to slip beneath the white quilt, the sheets and the bed's other accoutrements.

10

As we all know, the hours that pass never return and although the two people in the bed have no reason to regret this fact, quite the contrary – they're grateful, gorged and deep asleep – the guard outside will certainly get a shock when he wakes up. Because he too has fallen asleep, forgetting his duty and all his good intentions, and a real misfortune has befallen him. Irreparable.

For, taking advantage of his defenceless state, taking advantage of the fact that he was unable to fall asleep standing up in the middle of the field the way horses do, but instead had leaned gently back against the chain-link fence for some support, the people of the shanty town have relieved him of his regulation uniform. A quite unimaginable misfortune unless you bear in mind how skilled those hands are at picking pockets, how extraordinarily adept and discreet they are when it comes to appropriating other people's property. Everyone has to earn a living. Each person takes what is within his reach, you have only to read the newspapers to understand that. Not that newspapers themselves are an appropriation of other people's property: they're abandoned as useless only a few hours after being born. The people on the other side of the fence use them to keep warm, but first they pick up a few tips. Many are educated, they simply lack the means to put that education to use, but this is not to excuse the good guys who made off with the guard's uniform, it's simply a marginal note on the pragmatism of the needy, the same people who have now gone to their beds with a clear conscience and the certainty that at some point that uniform will come in handy.

It's beginning to grow light, timidly at first, the fingers of dawn as gentle as the first caressing touch of the fingers that touched the Señora or like the fingers that undressed the soldier, button by button, through the chain-link fence and made off, as if by magic, first with his kepi, then with his jacket, his shirt, his belt, his holster and, finally, his trousers, a manoeuvre that was an adventure in itself.

In the first light of day, everyone everywhere feels like sleeping on: under the roof of the club or the barracks – whichever you want to call it – out in the open, or half out in the open in the shanty dwell-

ings. They want to sleep but duty calls and the first
to wake is the intruder in Sleeping Beauty's bed. He
jumps out and carefully pulls the sheets back over her,
tucking her in.

'Don't catch cold, love, I don't want you getting
pneumonia. It's no joke trying to get hold of anti-
biotics.'

To which she replies, purring, barely opening her
eyes:

'If I fall ill, you can make me better. That's what
doctors are for.'

But Alfredi is already putting on the check shirt he
left draped over the chair.

'I ain't no doctor now, honey, you're gettin' all con-
fused. Anyway I gotta go.'

He jams his cap on at a jaunty angle. 'I gotta get
back to the cab,' he says, by way of explanation, 'or
d'you think I just sit on my butt all day with time to
spend pissing around here? Come on, move yourself,
I'm starving, gimme some coffee.'

'I haven't got any coffee. They cleaned me out, they
took the lot, the poor things. Anyway, you know I
can't get up. I've got willow sickness.'

The idea tickles her, she laughs, but he's in no mood
for jokes.

'The cab is waiting, woman, so don't you get funny
with me. Just be grateful I'm not one of the unem-
ployed.'

His tone of voice is not that of the previous night,
nor are his attitude, his gestures or his body language,
as they would have said on one of those drama courses

the Señora took before leaving the country, before she was a 'Señora' and long, long, long before she got into that bed.

This morning, wearing his daytime face, he's a taxi driver and he's shaking her by the arm and demanding his breakfast. Come on, he says. She's annoyed.

'Calm down. You weren't like this last night, you were sweet then, you were great. Don't mess me around. I can't stand bossy men.'

Today's man has a very short fuse and despises tarts who play hard to get. For that very reason, he shoves her back on to the bed, pushing the covers aside with one hand while lifting her nightdress with the other. He unzips his flies, does what he can without paying too much attention to detail, gives a few thrusts and is done.

'That's just so you'll remember the kind of man I am,' he explains to her as he stands up and adjusts his clothing, pulling on his cap. 'Actions not words, that's me.'

He exemplifies this with a small, obscene, very deliberate gesture, which consists of holding up one clenched fist and moving his wrist lightly back and forth.

'I get enough words in the cab. The crap I have to listen to just to pay the rent . . . anyone would think I was paid to listen.'

While he talks, he's tucking the tail of his check shirt inside his trousers and doing his flies up. Hurriedly, efficiently.

'Everybody's up to their neck in problems these

days and I gotta listen to them all, not only that, I'm expected to dole out free advice too. Every passenger who gets in thinks he's got the right to fill my head with his problems. I don't expect to have to listen to no one when I get home.'

'This isn't your home, pal,' says the Señora bluntly.

'It's as good as. Wherever I have a fuck, that's my home.'

'If you call what you've just done fucking . . .'

'You're just a castrating bitch like all women. I get plenty of them in the cab. Too many. See you tomorrow morning, babe. And don't forget the coffee.'

The Señora lets him know, in no uncertain terms, that she is not prepared to receive him in that frame of mind. It's the doctor I want to see, she says. Tell him to come tonight. If he doesn't, I might start forgetting again.

61

'Forget as much as you like, I don't care. All I need to remember is the address passengers give when they get in the cab,' says the cab driver conscientiously, swaggering towards the door.

11

Dawn has brought confusion to the military camp that surrounds the bungalow and at times includes it because, during the change of guard, the night guard has been discovered in his underwear, villainously stripped of his regulation uniform. It's easy to imagine the fury and embarrassment felt by Major Vento and his underlings. Orders, counterorders and insults fill the air. The guard probably wishes he'd never been born, and even if he doesn't now, the military gentlemen will soon make sure he does, for they're already devising an appropriate punishment. The incursions into the shanty town, whence the thieves doubtless came (they attacked me, they attacked me, shouts the guard, but no one believes him) have to be postponed for the moment, given the fact that the manoeuvres

being carried out at the country club are still top
secret. But the time for vengeance will come, as it will
for other acts of retaliation and revenge.

None of these vicissitudes concerns the Señora, or
rather she thinks they don't; she doesn't want them
to. She covers her head with the pillow and tries to
go back to sleep, which she certainly needs after the
ferment of last night. That's why she doesn't hear
the insistent knocking at the door. Or perhaps it just
gets mixed up with the noise coming from outside the
French windows, the noise of someone being struck.

And since the Señora does not reply, María decides
to go in anyway, using the master key as she has
on other occasions, and this time she's sure she'll be
welcome because she comes bearing a breakfast tray,
with a steaming cup of coffee and a plate with six
small croissants on it. Seeing that the Señora is asleep,
she puts the tray down on the left side of the bed and
runs on tiptoe to draw the curtains on the right. As
soon as she begins drawing the curtains, trying hard
not to make any noise, the Señora wakes up.

'What are you doing, María?' she asks, not noticing
the hand that reaches slowly out from beneath her
bed to the plate. The hand grabs two of the croissants
and immediately disappears.

'Nothing, Señora, nothing,' María inevitably replies.
'Good morning, Señora. You were asleep and I
thought the light might be bothering you.'

The light isn't bothering me, but a lot of other
things are, the Señora thinks to herself, but all she
says to María is: 'Leave those curtains alone, María.'

She says it with a defiant look.

But nobody can beat María when it comes to facing down defiant looks. Or when it comes to active defiance, and she goes on drawing the curtains as if she hadn't heard, blocking the view. The same view which, up until that precise moment, the Señora had wanted to remove from her consciousness but which now suddenly arouses her intense interest.

'Will you leave the curtains alone!' insists the Señora. And seeing that her words have little effect, she tries a threat:

'If you don't do as I say . . . If you don't do as I say, I'm going to have to, have to . . . do something.'

María obeys instantly.

'Of course, Señora. Whatever you want, Señora. I've brought you some breakfast. Milky coffee and half a dozen fresh, crisp croissants.'

65

She's barely finished speaking when the hand reappears from beneath the bed and carries off the last of the croissants.

'The lady in bungalow 27 ordered them, the one who's got the Olympic-size swimming pool, and I took a few of them for you. I know the baker,' María explains helpfully, so that the Señora can appreciate the full measure of her sphere of influence.

'You owe me 13,000,' she adds, because it's one thing having influence, but quite another giving things away for free.

The Señora, who's basically a realist, looks at the empty plate and asks what croissants she's talking about.

María washes her hands of the matter.

'I don't know anything about that. I just know I brought you half a dozen croissants. Six nice, crisp croissants. That's 13,000 in local currency. Or rather, that's how much they cost at seven o'clock this morning when the baker handed them to me. It's now half past eight. The price must have gone up to about 14,200 by now.'

'Leave me in peace!'

Peace. That certainly doesn't seem to be the watchword outside the French windows, neither on this nor the other side of the fence. There is feverish activity outside, in this small but intense part of the world. On the manicured lawn, which is now rather less manicured, the soldiers are venting their rage by marching martially, furiously, up and down. They come and go in a display of strength intended to frighten the onlookers. Only a few of the latter are male and they're all very young, there are more women than men, but they are neither very afraid nor, strictly speaking, onlookers, since they're busy paraphrasing and parodying the parade, walking up and down the bare field on the other side of the barbed-wire fence, brooms at the ready as if they were rifles.

The Major shouts orders at the marching soldiers: About turn!

Ta-a-ke aim! and the soldiers aim their rifles at their irreverent female counterparts. The latter are not so easily intimidated. They lay down their brooms and pick up old saucepans, badly dented from frequent use, on this as on other such occasions, as deafening drums. They bang gleefully away on them.

'What's going on outside?' asks the Señora from her vast bed, alarmed.

'It seems there was a mutiny, an act of insubordination. That rabble out there are always so uppity; they've no respect for order, restraint. But don't you worry, Señora, the military gentlemen know how to keep the plebs under control. I'll turn the TV on, that's much nicer. I'll choose a good channel.'

María draws the remote control out of her pocket as if from a holster. She wields it like a weapon. Ta-a-ke aim ... she says, a familiar inflection in her voice. And then: Fire!

The television responds as if by magic – electronic magic. Folk dances invade the room with images and sound.

The Señora, who has discovered the power of the threat, uses it:

'I've told you before, María ...'

'All right, I'll switch it off. Don't threaten me. Just pay me the 15,000 you owe me and I'll go. I've got a lot to do, you know.'

'What 15,000?'

'I've told you already, for the croissants.'

The Señora seems perplexed, she points to the tray.

'I didn't even *see* a croissant. I didn't even eat them. What are you charging me for then? Are there any croissants here? Besides, when all this began, it was 13,000 not 15,000.'

'That was when I first brought them in,' protests

María. 'You should have paid me then instead of wasting time arguing. Because,' and she says this proudly, drawing herself up, 'that's what hyperinflation does, Señora, we can't waste any time here. It's 15,000 now and you'd better hurry before it goes up again.'

The Señora doesn't find such jokes in the least bit funny. She tells María that she should be ashamed of abusing her in this way and making fun of the country's extremely grave economic problems. María protests. Nothing she does or says is a joke, and to prove it she's going to call Major Vento.

'Call who you like. You wouldn't take any notice, even if I told you not to . . .'

María is pleased by these words. She feels acknowledged. Just as well the Señora has realized that she, María, is no longer the woman she was. She's been receiving training from the military gentlemen out there, not systematically, but artfully, and she now knows how to defend herself against any attack, verbal or otherwise. She's learned counterinsurgency and non-conventional warfare techniques. She has become 'tough, astute and bold' as recommended in the Manual, which she now knows by heart.

'I'm going to tell Major Vento,' she says, by way of a threat, as she goes out through the French windows towards the golf course.

12

'. . . oissants and she doesn't want to pay for them,'
María is saying to the Major when they both appear
through the French windows and enter the room.

The Señora doesn't know whether to laugh, cry,
hide under the covers or scream blue murder. She
only knows that she's not going to be able to get up,
that she's certainly not going to die with her boots on.
Nor even with her slippers on.

The Major has not even deigned to look at her, yet.
He's talking to María.

'You were quite right to alert me, Corporal. Things
mustn't be allowed to get out of hand here. Here,
order must reign, here, we must all work as a team.
Every minute of the day we face new challenges.'

The Señora is distracted from the disquiet that all

this might otherwise provoke in her by the discovery of a rather timid hand that creeps out cautiously from beneath her bed and makes off with the cup of coffee without spilling a drop.

She can't contain her surprise.

'A hand!' she cries.

A good pretext for the Major to smooth his moustaches.

'A hand? Explain yourself, Señora.'

'I saw a hand. It took my cup. They must have taken the croissants too. They take everything.'

'Affirmative, Señora. Absolutely. They take everything. It's just typical of the now obsolete Left, intended to spread unrest among the people. They take everything, they're the ones that cause the shortages. They'll do anything to destabilize the system and stay alive. They steal food, they incite the needy classes to plunder supermarkets and, even worse, the government does nothing, takes no steps against it at all. Our duty, therefore, is to change the government.'

He looks at María, who gives a satisfied nod. He smoothes his moustaches again and makes his declaration of faith.

'The left is a running sore.'

Possibly with the ignoble purpose of contradicting him, the same hand that provoked the peroration reappears to return the cup. It replaces it on its saucer on the tray at the foot of the bed. The cup is empty.

Strange though it may seem, this fact calms the Señora.

'With all due respect, sir, you're wrong. It wasn't

the left. It was, without a shadow of a doubt, the right.'

'This country is plagued with dangerous looters and left-wing agitators who profit from the difficult social situation the people are in at the moment. But don't worry, *we* will soon be taking steps to avoid any uprising.'

'You mean you're going to resolve the people's difficulties?'

'Of course not. We're going to crush the malcontents.'

The Señora feels she has the right to object.

'Shut up, Señora, and don't answer back. You know nothing, you see nothing. It suits you to conform to the stereotype. You're obviously a left-wing sympathizer, a bit of an idiot – like all women, in my opinion.'

María, who is drinking from the sweet chalice of the Major's words, stands to attention. He continues:

'We,' he says, pointing to himself, 'are quite capable of healing this running sore. All the trouble here is caused by the left. You're the ones who want to make us believe that in this extremely wealthy country – where cows were once slaughtered merely for their tongues – there is now hunger. When we take over we will pass a decree proving the contrary to be true.'

'Lately . . . ,' the stubborn Señora begins.

'There is no lately. This regiment here will take power, come hell or high water, we'll take on the Air Force and the Navy and any part of the Army who elect not to support us – poor wretches. We'll get rid

71

once and for all of the malcontents, the depressed, the professional moaners and the rebels! The rebels too, so you be careful . . . Pay this worthy representative of the working classes what you owe her and we can get on with our lives in peace, if you'll pardon the expression.'

Swift as an arrow, María says that the debt has now risen to 27,000.

The Señora makes no move to obey. The Major does not appreciate this display of passive disobedience.

'I've told you once and I won't tell you again. Pay up and don't play into the hands of the left.'

'It was the right hand, I saw it clearly. I remember it well.'

'Remembering is not advisable,' pronounces the man in uniform.

María, her eye on the clock, is attending to her own interests.

'It's 27,600, 700, 800. At ten o'clock in the morning exactly, the half dozen croissants (category: manufactured goods) are valued at 28,000 on the stock exchange. And rising.'

Anyone who has chosen to ensconce herself in bed and is prepared to defend her position against whatever vicissitudes fate may throw at her, however unexpected, must learn to practise resignation, at least when no other option presents itself. The Señora senses she's fighting a losing battle and reaches out to pick up her wallet. Her hand is not the only one looking for her purse. Other hands immediately appear, large, hairy hands and smaller but equally industrious hands. They're the same hands as before, but now they shake and writhe like small, carnivorous plants. They want to reach the wallet but fail to do so; from her advance position on the bed, the Señora has the advantage over them, the hands are active but timid, they're only willing to reveal a small part of their arm, they've no intention of coming out into the open. Among the folds of eiderdown and lace-trimmed sheets there are hands and hands only, all trying to grab the wallet that the Señora has now picked up in order to take out the money which she immediately hands over to María.

Major Vento, standing to attention, pretends not to notice. What can one man without his machine gun do against so many snake-like hands, a bit like the head of that gorgon creature?

The Señora, however, feels more relaxed and is beginning to enjoy herself.

'I'm not used to this. It's so different. I mean, I've just come from a city where the most extraordinary things happen, but nothing like this.'

The Major takes her remark as a compliment.

'This is the best country in the world and we're about to prove it to you, the new history begins with us. The best country in the world, you'll see.'

'Well, it's certainly very fetching.'

'You don't think we're serious, but you'll see,' blusters Major Vento, losing his military composure. 'You'll see, when the social timebomb explodes and they can do nothing to control it. They're going to have to beg us for help on their bended knees, you'll see. The government out there is busy manufacturing rubber bullets, tear gas. I'd laugh, if it wasn't so sad. Rubber bullets, I ask you! We, on the other hand, are well equipped. "We have the brain, the heart, and the muscle to make things happen. Any powerful weapon is merely an extension of ourselves," as it says in the Manual. We're a crack regiment, we know what bullets to use and they're all high calibre. Very high calibre, believe me.'

It may be an involuntary action due to a slight itching not at all at odds with an otherwise iron discipline, but the fact is that, while uttering these final words, Major Vento is fingering his crotch, albeit reasonably discreetly. But there is nothing discreet, quite the opposite, about the way he approaches the bed and, by the same token, the Señora lying on it.

María reminds him of the restraint demanded by his mission.

'Major,' she murmurs, and touches his shoulder. 'Come on, Major,' she says again.

The Major looks at her surprised, as if caught *in flagrante*; but he recovers himself.

He does an about turn and escorts María towards the French windows. She holds out some money in notes to him. He exits and she turns triumphantly to the Señora.

'And to think that you had me believing you were best friends with, at the very least, a colonel.'

And to emphasize her words and her displeasure, she grabs the remote control and switches on the TV again; then, in disgust, she picks up the empty tray from the bed and flounces out.

13

Exquisite images of the capital appear on the giant television screen which occupies almost the whole of one wall: flowering chorisia trees, jacarandas in bloom (that most intense of purples), tree-lined streets and parks so splendid they seem almost incongruous. There are clean streets full of happy passers-by and restaurants built in large old houses that are certain people's idea of bliss, there's no sign of trash cans or homeless people scavenging in them or . . .

The Señora can take no more and she suddenly bursts into tears. She cries, sobbing loudly, uncontrollably. She throws herself down on the bed, helpless, and gives full vent to her tears, which flow like the waters of a fountain. She doesn't notice the two hands that come creeping out from between the folds of the valance and grasp the edge of the bed. She doesn't notice the close-cropped head that appears behind the hands, nor the bright eyes beneath the brief thatch of hair. It's Lucho, the conscript forced to drag himself along on his elbows, the same conscript who was punished by being buried in the ground, who has managed to escape the oppressive pit and would now like to console her.

'Don't cry, Señora. Why are you crying?'

A good question. She tries to pull herself together and answer it with the seriousness it merits.

'That was my city, the one on the TV. This new city isn't the one I used to know, they've changed everything. Now I don't know who the enemy is, I don't know who to fight against. Before I went away I did, now the enemy's no longer there, or at least he says he isn't, but he is and I just don't know where I stand.'

Actually you're lying down, Lucho reminds her sensibly.

Exactly, replies the Señora, unhelpfully, and starts to cry again.

'Señora,' Lucho tries to bring her back to reality, 'Señora.'

'I came back to find *that* not *this*. I came back to recover my memory and they steal it from me, erase it. They sweep it away. And what if lying in a strange bed unable to move was my way of preserving my memory and everything else they're busy snatching away from us, by dint of taking the bread out of our mouths? And there was so much bread then, so much wine,' the Señora snivels. 'I'm crying because I don't understand anything,' she adds.

'Oh well,' Lucho says, reassured. 'If that's all it is, then we should all be crying. But here we are. Not understanding is no reason to cry.'

'It isn't? Maybe I'm crying because I'm suffering from "willow sickness", as a doctor friend here diagnosed. *I* must have "weeping willow sickness".'

'If it was Dr Alfredi who told you, that throws a different light on the matter. Alfredi knows everything. He can solve any problem, you'll see. I thought you were crying because I stole your croissants. That really is serious. I'm very sorry. Will you forgive me? If I'd known they were going to be so expensive, I'd have come straight out and asked you for the money.'

'Inflation's very high.'

'Yes, but with me you would have been investing the money. I'd have put it into bonds.'

The subject of money bores the Señora, coming as she does from other latitudes. She prefers to ask the pleasant head sticking out from beneath her bed:

'What's your name?'

Lucho bows, as best he can from such an awkward position, and recites:

'Conscript José Luis Gutiérrez, company three, regiment eight of the infantry, on manoeuvres on the golf course of Las Ranas country club, presently headquarters of the commandos, reporting ... at home they call me Lucho.'

This last remark, said in a sweet, almost childish voice, awakens in the Señora an almost maternal instinct she had not suspected she harboured in her world-weary heart inured to all these changes in climate and customs. It must be to do with coming back home, back to certain unexpectedly familiar undertones, she tells herself, while saying to conscript José Luis Gutiérrez, from company three, regiment eight, etc:

'Come out here, Lucho. Don't stay down there. You look like the Aztec Flower.'

And she laughs. The boy probably doesn't know what she's talking about. She's obviously absorbed in memories of her youth, in recollections. It was the disembodied head that used to appear on a table in the old Retiro Park; it was a fairground trick, she explains, just in case.

'Hardly anyone goes to the fairground now, there's no money,' he says nostalgically.

'Lucho,' says the Señora, softening. 'Come out from under there, Lucho.'

He shakes his head, no, no, says the head.

'I can't,' adds his mouth. 'I'm doing my military service.'

'Military service? Where? In the undercover navy?'

She can hear that outside, after mature reflection by his superiors, the soldier who went to sleep while guarding the prisoner is being made an example of, which is why everyone has forgotten about the prisoner. She can hear the crack of the whip, as well as other even fiercer disciplinary measures being applied, measures that make no sound. Crack, again, crack, accompanied by the cry of 'Insubordinate!' and then

'Rebel!' and 'Slacker!' Traitor, turncoat, leftie, are other words brought into play in a situation which, for the protagonist, is not in the least playful.

Lucho understands what's happening and quickly disappears beneath the bed. The Señora, who has lived abroad for the last ten years, seems unalarmed. She lies prone on the bed and tries to peer underneath.

'What are you doing down there? Digging trenches?' she asks in a low voice.

Lucho pokes his nose out, the bare minimum, puts his finger to his lips and says Shhh.

She feels like playing and signals to him to come out again. She makes it clear that she'll do her best to protect him, that he needn't be afraid with her there. Lucho knows that in these circumstances he's not going to get very far anyway, even if he wanted to, and so he emerges from his hiding place, completely naked, as naked as the day he was born, or rather as naked as the day the military gentlemen punished him by burying him in a pit. Without a moment's delay (contrary to what one might expect), the Señora lifts up the coverlet and invites him to lie down – under the quilt but on top of the covers. She doesn't want him to get the wrong idea.

'The people from the shanty town took all your clothes,' she remarks dispassionately.

'No,' he says, 'they didn't take mine. It was the army who punished me. It's all part of being a soldier. They assume that sooner or later everyone gets taken prisoner. You have to learn the hard way, they say.'

'I see.'

'No, you don't see anything. You see nothing, saw nothing, will see nothing. If you do see anything, they'll kill you. They're dangerous, be careful. They're not playing. They're aiming to save the country by kicking it into shape.'

The idea fills the Señora with unbearable sadness and she starts to cry again. The young soldier by her side in bed doesn't know what to say to console her.

'Don't cry any more. Please. I can't bear it when you cry. Maybe you're hungry. And I stole your croissants. I gave two to my sister, to poor Patri. They hadn't eaten in the shanty town for three days until you got here. You should be happy.'

'You're right. If I can help at all . . .'

'You can't help now, now you're hungry too. But we're going to get some meat soon. Don't worry so much, your hunger will soon go away.'

The Señora feels terribly sad.

'If only I were hungry like you. That would be true solidarity.'

'What do you mean? Now everyone's hungry. That's how things are.'

'There never used to be hunger in this country, there was always more than enough to eat.'

'You mean in *our* country.'

'I . . . it's as if I wasn't from here. I feel such an outsider, I don't understand anything. I need time to orient myself, to tie up loose ends. I don't know. I've come from so far away.'

'Where are you from then?'

'I'm from here. But I left ten years ago during the

military dictatorship and I thought that coming back to a democracy everything would be much simpler.'

Lucho, leaning on one elbow facing the Señora, lets himself drop on to the pillow.

'I don't know anything about all that. I'm just doing my military service, they don't let us think about details like that.'

'Mine's a kind of military service too. Part of Operation Return. I thought I was coming to this country club to rest, to readjust. Perhaps there's something else too . . .'

'Perhaps. I've no idea, I'm just a conscript.'

83

14

The sounds coming in through the window have varied in both emotional and acoustic intensity. The fury unleashed against the unworthy guard has subsided for some reason and is gradually replaced by more muffled (but suitably military) sounds, of horses and steel.

Lucho and the Señora continue talking, fairly animatedly given the circumstances, until they hear a thud, hard enough to make the bed tremble slightly, accompanied by more insults and shouts, apparently expressing both alarm and encouragement: Come on, Apollo, get up!

The more distant cries, almost simultaneous with the others, are cries of triumph.

Lucho immediately pricks up his ears and raises himself up on one elbow.

'That's it. They've done it at last. I hope my sister gets a piece of sirloin.'

'Sirloin?' asks the Señora.

'Yes, from the horse. They say horse meat's very nutritious. The horse belonging to the military, it dropped down dead, didn't you hear it? Our boys will be carving it up already. They were all prepared, some of them even had their knives sharpened and ready. Make sure you get some sirloin, Patri!'

'You're all mad.'

'No, we're just hungry.'

'I'm sorry,' says the Señora. 'I'm sorry.'

'Don't worry, there'll be enough meat for everyone, if they act quickly. There are more and more of us in the shanty town. A lot of people with nowhere to live in the city come here. We welcome them, not like in some other shanty towns where they put up notices saying: "Middle classes go home". Even some people from the club have ended up there, Major Vento's throwing them out . . .'

'Something should be done about it,' says the Señora, without knowing quite what.

'Yes it should, but go on with what you were telling me before.'

On the golf course, the military gentlemen are screaming: Vultures! Sharks! Hyenas! They shout at the people and try to beat them back with their rifle butts, but the 'butchering gang' are in full swing. Vultures, cry the would-be repressors and, against all logic, it's clear that they're referring to the others, the hungry ones. One of them does manage to mutter a gloomy prayer: Poor Apollo, he was worn out, we worked him too hard. He did his duty, says another steadier voice, he died like a soldier. Butchered by enemy hands, wails the first mourner. That is a misfortune that no longer concerns you, the steady voice declares sternly.

Above all the hubbub the calm voice of Major Vento is heard saying that this cannot be tolerated. That law and order no longer exist. That the people have made fools of them and thereby of all the armed forces in the country and that, given the government's impotence, its inability to command respect, it's up to them to do a thorough job of it.

His words must have been accompanied by some gesture because a detachment of soldiers suddenly bursts in through the French windows.

Lucho immediately disappears beneath the blanket. He slides slowly down, covered by the bedclothes, like a great white worm, and crawls under the bed again.

The soldiers are followed into the room by Major Vento and his ADC, without asking permission, without even glancing at the Señora, who observes them with a look of defiance and bewilderment.

The ADC speaks first. They've gone too far this time, he complains.

'Which is why the time has come for action,' says the Major. 'We'll take to the streets, we'll march on Government House.'

Major Vento is convinced that they'll gladly hand

over power to him. Because he'll arrive with his crack regiment trained for the job, not like those poor starving soldiers languishing in the barracks. Crack troops who know the Manual from cover to cover, from right to, no sorry, from back to, no not that either, who know the Manual as well as if they'd written it themselves. They've also read *Commandos in Action*, they know it by heart, they've practised the toughest combat exercises. Besides, they'll be happy to hand over power to us, because the government must be aware that we're on the verge of an outbreak of social unrest.

'And if the government does nothing to stop the restless hordes, our duty is to intervene.'

88   The ADC is not as confident as the Major.

'Do you think so? Let's wait a bit, give it some more thought.'

The Major stands to attention, clicks his heels:

'The army doesn't hesitate, it acts. Remember, sir, remember those wise words: doubt is a concept for intellectuals. Or for female intellectuals like the one lying on the bed over there pretending not to listen. But we know she's watching us and admiring us, aren't you, darling? She admires us and will join us when the time comes. She knows which is the winning side.'

He gives the Señora a wink, turns away before he can catch her look of disgust and walks towards the French windows to summon his troops.

15

The troops, although the word 'troupe' also springs to mind (they are so few in number), heed his call, and there is something of the pack about them too, a pack of panting dogs perhaps, begging for a sugar lump. They're touching in a way, or so they seem to the blonde Señora, who allows them to invade the room without even a word being exchanged. She doesn't protest and they clearly think it unnecessary to ask her permission, or to say sorry or even good morning. Their gaze is fixed on their natural leaders and she screws up her eyes trying to understand. There's something familiar about all this, although not perhaps as experienced by her. There's something on the edge of her memory trying to find expression and she both wants and doesn't want to recover it

Yes, she does want to and she struggles to do so, knowing how important, indeed vital, it is, and lying very still with her eyes closed, she senses that she will be able to put herself back together again, to find all the pieces of an internal jigsaw puzzle and that her memory will then help her to understand a little of this whole incongruous business.

Major Vento seems unwilling to allow her to concentrate, or even to keep her eyes shut. On guard! he shouts, to his men of course, but his voice is so loud and so penetrating that she feels it right in her solar plexus and sits up straight.

Attention! About turn! March!

The march proceeds from one corner to the other of the somewhat limited space, which is large for a bungalow in a country club but much too small to be a parade ground.

This is better than TV, the Señora consoles herself, resigned now to being a captive audience. Better than TV, anything's better than that, she says, as if trying to convince herself, giving a sideways glance at the vast screen that is still spewing out its now predictable stream of trivia.

In the room, on the other hand, the action has changed from image to sound, for Major Vento has told his troops to stand at ease and is now haranguing them.

'We are a new type of soldier with new weaponry and a new sense of motivation. Our mission is to act swiftly to demoralize, disrupt and destroy the enemy.

Now we need to make ourselves easily identifiable, we need to stand out from the crowd. We are unique!'

16

Operation Identity is being carried out with great speed, order and decorum. There was initial confusion when the ADC came up with the idea of using burnt cork and promptly sailed off to the officers' mess where he found a good supply. Battle camouflage was the order of the day, but as the day wore on, a touch of vanity entered the proceedings.

The Señora almost expects them to ask her if they can borrow her eyebrow pencil, but no, they don't go that far, although they are looking lovely. They make each other up almost affectionately. One says to his companion: Put a bit more black here to make my nose look thinner; another cries: No, no, wipe that off, I can't abide symmetry. They all crowd and shove each other in front of the large wardrobe mirror, someone says: Hasn't anyone got a hand mirror? I want to see how I look from the back. The Señora is enjoying herself. She's considering offering them her eyebrow pencil anyway so that they can draw lines around the black smudges on their faces. Because of their mottled appearance, she's almost about to call them dalmatians, pointers. Fortunately, she's distracted by a voice to her left, that of the television, which is no longer the cooing voice of a few moments ago, but that of an alarmed announcer, intercut with the hiss of interference.

'Military uprising / in regiment eight / of the infantry recen / tly billeted /for security reasons in / the country club Las / Ranas.'

94

The announcer's head comes and goes on the screen among zigzagging lines.

In the (let's call it) barracks, the soldiers have finished applying their makeup, sorry, their identifying camouflage. The Señora casts an appraising eye over them: they've created quite an interesting look, they wouldn't be out of place in a film about Vietnam, fighting in the jungle in full regalia.

The Señora tries to get her brain into gear in order to jumpstart the neurones that deal with historical reconstruction or with constitutional law or whatever it is that she needs if she's to see clearly. She closes her eyes tight shut and is possibly on the verge of getting a glimmer of something that might help explain the events she's an involuntary witness to – the cyclical pattern of horror, as she seriously suspects

– when the phone rings and shatters her concentration.

Not that of the troops, though; they remain concentrated, crouching, ready to bound forward as one man, feline and disciplined.

The Señora has picked up the receiver, she's said hello, but the voice at the other end is not interested in polite exchanges.

'We're gonna get you. Get out of that bed 'cause we're gonna get you. We know everything. We know what your mission is. You're after your memory, but we're gonna get you first. History begins with us,' says a distorted voice which, despite the distortion and the bad connection, appears to be that of María the maid.

The Señora is no longer in the least amused by what's going on. She drops the phone as if it had bitten her and tries to hide beneath the bedclothes.

The blackened troops have no time for wimps. In practice for combat, one of the soldiers leaps over the Señora's bed and, in doing so, tears back the blanket covering her face with his bayonet. Others at her feet line up to perform squats and jumps, leaping higher and higher like ever larger and more frightening amphibians; one after another, mouths gaping, they leap the obstacle that is her bed.

The Señora wants to get up, galvanized into action at last. She wants to run away but the soldiers flying over her, like the sheep you count to get to sleep, won't let her.

So the Señora stays there, frozen amid the fine linen sheets and the lace trimmings, rather as if wrapped in a shroud, and she knows the only way out of this situation is to recover her power of speech like someone recovering a lost memory. And they won't let her, they won't let her. Just when she's about to think, just when she's about to put a thought into words, one of them brushes her nose with the butt of a rifle or gleefully crushes her against the bed.

She stays there, terrified, trying to disappear beneath the white bedclothes.

That's why she doesn't notice that some of them have brought with them helmets covered in netting and that others have plucked the few remaining branches from the hedge growing by the chain-link fence and are arranging them on their helmets, weaving them into the netting. With this extra camouflage the soldiers are ready for action. They stand to attention.

'The rebels are on a war footing!' thunders the announcer's voice from the giant screen, having overcome the interference. 'They are threatening to march on the capital. This could very well unleash a civil war.'

Tolerance has its limits, and one of the soldiers, duly equipped and differentiated, gives the screen a kick, shouting:

'What do you mean "*civil* war"; we're the military!'

The broadcast is interrupted thanks to the efficacy of the punishment meted out. There are now only zigzagging lines and winking lights.

17

During this parade of eccentricities, the people from the shanty town have been gathering, pressing up against the chain-link fence. There are a lot of them now, women and men and children and old people and dogs and. Things start hotting up.

'Hey, woody!' they start shouting at the soldiers with twigs in their helmets. 'What are you supposed to be?'

'You'd better get down to the cleaners sharpish!'

'A clear case of psoriasis!' cry the better informed among them. 'Try using soap!' shout others. 'Bring on the carnival floats!' they cry in unison and that seems the most popular idea. 'What do we want? Carnival floats! When do we want them? Now!'

The Señora in her bed, which is like a boat adrift

on troubled waters, peers out from beneath the covers. I like carnival, it reminds me of . . . she starts to say almost out loud, loud enough to be heard, but Major Vento once more seals her lips.

'Soldiers! Attention!' howls Major Vento, and it is unclear as to whether or not he means to include the Señora in that order.

She keeps very quiet, just in case.

The soldiers, on the other hand, fall in to form a compact group.

'Tanks out!' roars the Major.

Just this once, and with all the respect due to his superior, the ADC remarks:

'We haven't actually got any tanks here, Major.'

98   And without a pause between word and action, he slaps a couple of stripes on the Major's epaulette.

'Colonel,' he says and then, adding yet another stripe, 'General!'

The troops are fascinated by this promotion, instant as cup-a-soup. They stand to attention, salute in rigorous unison and begin to sing the national anthem.

'The tanks, yes sir,' insists the Major. 'The ones we use on military manoeuvres in the bunkers.'

The mere mention fills the ADC with enthusiasm.

'In the bunkers, on the greens. At the 19th hole!'

The soldiers, ready to obey the least of the Major's orders – his will is their desire – rush off in search of the tanks used in manoeuvres and return shortly afterwards with the caddy-carts, inoffensive-looking motorized golf carts.

As for the Señora – who in her USA existence

naturally had her moment of glory in Hollywood –
she can't decide if she's in a Spielberg movie or a Walt
Disney production. To make sure, she peers out in
her usual hesitant way, trying not to make herself too
conspicuous, and she sees the military gentlemen, fully
deployed, driving round her room in their tiny golf
carts, fired by enthusiasm for the cause, preparing
themselves for the glorious destiny that awaits them.

The carts go round and round, faster and faster,
crashing into each other. It's like being at the funfair.
Some of the drivers decorate the aforementioned golf
carts with camouflage blacking and the last of the
twigs torn from the hedge.

For a moment the Señora feels she finally has the
strength and resolve to jump out of bed and run
away. The soldiers, in various capacities and wildly
differing poses (threatening, persuasive, rejecting,
commanding) prevent her from acting on this emi-
nently sensible decision. More than once, in a state of
some confusion, she asks herself, Can this be real or
am I dreaming it? And while, on the one hand, she
knows she can't be dreaming it, on the other, she suspects that had she not drawn the curtains at a certain
point in her life she would not now for one moment
doubt that all this was happening.

The Señora in her bed in the middle of this room
invaded by soldiers prepared for war may seem both
passive – although not unreflecting – and intimidated.
A reaction typical of the idle rich. The plebs on the
other side of the fence do not even know the meaning

of the word 'intimidate' and they spare no effort in mocking these noble servants of the Fatherland.

After what we might call a reasonable interval – about ten minutes – the soldiery, in response to the escalation in verbal aggression: insults, mockery, taunts, sarcasm, jeers, attacks, offensive remarks, gibes, exclamations, expletives ('Blacking is for boots, you jerks, not your face!' is the kindest thing that has so far been shouted at them), erupt into action and lash out at the mob.

The chain-link fence acts as a barricade.

Having lost everything, the people from the shanty town fear nothing, not even bullets, and are roaring with laughter.

100 The soldiers, who do not know what it is to lose (or to win for that matter) are afraid of the laughter. They're bewildered.

Back in the Señora's room, which is now their general headquarters, the ringing of the telephone calls them all to order.

The Señora picks up the receiver.

'Hello,' she says, only to hear the same distorted voice which, she would swear, is María's.

'We're gonna get you. You think too much, we know who your cronies are, we're gonna . . .'

Furious, the Señora again slams down the phone, a gesture that seems cyclical, inevitable. The soldiers consider the real action to be outside now, not in this repetitive room. The stragglers depart with dignity and conviction. They depart with a clear vision of the mission that awaits them.

18

In the midst of all this turmoil, the Señora has not noticed that night has fallen. But it has and it's already pretty dark when she hears someone stealthily opening her door. She's frightened. Thinking it might be María, she quickly turns on the bedside light only to smile with relief when she recognizes Alfredi. And 'recognize' is the right word since the doctor-cum-taxi driver is at this point wearing a (clumsily applied) false white beard.

He rushes in looking dazed, his leather cap tipped towards his left ear and only the right sleeve of his doctor's gown on. He moves in haste, loses his cap, and finally manages to pull the gown on over his blue check shirt and button it up to the neck, adjusting his false beard. He smiles, calmer now.

The Señora, who's been watching him with some concern, smiles in turn when she sees that all trace of the cab driver has disappeared. She moves over as if to make room for him, but he sits down sedately at the foot of the bed.

'So you want to go back to dreaming in Spanish?' he asks.

'I don't know. I don't know anything any more.'

'Yes, you do. What do you associate with the word "gears"?'

'What do I associate . . .? Why? What do you care? Look, I've got more serious things wrong with me: a little pain here. Let's see now. Or is it here . . .'

But he's not so easily seduced.

'These physical pains are psychosomatic in origin. We need to find out what causes them. Tell me about your childhood.'

'When I was a little girl, my mummy . . . What is all this nonsense, doctor? Get to the point.'

Unruffled, he tells her that one can only gain access to the symbolic via the imaginary. Our dreams are the royal road to the unconscious, he tells her. We mustn't rush things, he says.

'That's not what you said last night.'

'Yesterday was different. I had a different role then. We mustn't get ourselves mixed up. There's a time and a place for everything.'

'How was the cab?'

'It was a source of great frustration today. No one takes cabs any more, not with the latest increase in fares, and the only passenger who got in had one of those brand-new 500,000 notes they've just issued. We couldn't get anyone to change it. There was no change to be had in the whole city: it was high value notes or nothing. So the passenger got out without paying. It's not worth driving around in conditions like that.'

'Just as well. I hated the cab driver. I like the doctor.'

'It's too early. It's only half past nine at night, it's not time for the doctor yet; it's all a question of circadian rhythms, you know.'

'So?' asks the Señora.

He sits up straight and proud.

'So now I'm a psychoanalyst: halfway between cabbie and doctor.'

103

Outside the French windows the shouts grow louder: insults from the people, threats from the soldiers. A few soldiers in the lower ranks peer through the window, as if wanting to come in. Alfredi whispers to the Señora, I'm your psychoanalyst, remember, your psychoanalyst! and setting his false beard straight, he solemnly goes over to the window and draws the curtains.

'Doctor, I feel like I'm being followed,' the Señora says to him when he returns to sit at the foot of the bed.

'What do you mean by that? Describe the feeling.'

'It's not so much a feeling as actual incidents.'

'Paranoia.'

'People keep phoning me, Doctor, and threatening me.'

'People don't always threaten you over the phone then?'

'No, not always. Only lately. They phone me up and threaten me.'

'And what do they say?'

'They say: "We're gonna get you".'

'That's all very subjective. It could mean get you out of bed, get you out of your rut, out of the rat race . . .'

The Señora shakes her head. No, no. She grows discouraged but the doctor insists.

'Or get you out of your nightdress perhaps. Like this?'

He may be suggestive in his new Freudian role but he's hardly innovative, as he once more begins by slipping off the shoulder straps of her nightdress and stroking her shoulder.

He's torn off his beard now, his gown is halfway down his chest and he's recovered the more informal air of the young doctor. And it's in his role as doctor that he says to the Señora:

'Now let me listen to your chest. That's it, put your little hand here; now open your mouth and breathe deeply.'

He gently squeezes her cheeks, pursing her lips, and kisses her. A brief kiss because, in his excitement, he needs both hands to remove the doctor's coat. He's then in the check shirt of the cab driver.

'Come on, sweetheart, do something, gimme a hand! I ain't got all night.'

She helps him remove the blue check shirt, in genuine haste: she wants nothing to do with the cabbie who emerges from beneath the doctor's white gown.

The Señora pulls off his shirt, helps him with his trousers and the doctor, I mean, plain Alfredi grows sweeter as he loses his clothes. Completely naked now, he slips hurriedly between the sheets. Just one thing bothers him. He ferrets among the bedclothes, finds it and hurls it away. It's the Manual that María so kindly lent the Señora.

19

The lovers have disappeared beneath the soft bedspread, which is now trembling, shaking and undulat-
ing in movements proper to this third act, which also
happens to be sexual.

The cries from the outside world do not reach the
ears of the lovers, isolated in their cave and concen-
trating on more pleasurable noises.

Outside, to cries of 'Deserter!', pandemonium
breaks out. The cause of this new and even more
febrile outbreak is Lucho, caught while running naked
to hide in the no man's land that is the shanty town.
Covered by what amounts almost to a firing squad,
Lucho has been forced to climb the chain-link fence,
carefully avoiding the barbed wire at the top, and to
return to the so-called barracks badly scratched.

Major Vento rounds on him:

'Here we are about to march towards glory and we already have a deserter, damn you!'

And he has the imaginative idea of ordering his men to crucify Lucho against the fence itself.

Lucho's feet are bound, his legs close together, and his arms are outstretched at shoulder height. The rope cuts into his ankles, into his wrists. 'Wrist,' he thinks, to keep his mind off what is happening, and stoically tries to withstand the ordeal. He doesn't actually know the word 'stoically', but he knows exactly what it means. As for the word 'ordeal', it would seem that he has just begun to learn its meaning, just a little, just the tip of it; later they will take pains to teach him its meaning inch by agonizing inch.

'Now you're going to get your just deserts,' the Major tells him, kicking him with one of his fine military boots.

And he announces to his troops that the prisoner is to stay there for the vultures to devour, while they're busy seizing power. We'll deal with him when the time comes, he adds. Meanwhile the prisoner can learn his lesson, for being a troublemaker and a rebel.

In the bungalow, in the bed, the tide is reaching its highest point.

Outside, against the fence, immobilized, Lucho is also shaking, writhing and trembling. They've left him alone; not one of the Major's – sorry, General's – men wants to miss the glorious fate awaiting them at the steps of Government House by having to stand guard over this soldier who is little better than trash.

Lucho twists and turns convulsively, but gets nowhere: the ropes are tied tight, they don't give at all, they just cut into him. To make doubly sure, they've handcuffed his outstretched arms to the fence, just in case, so that he can wait there, crucified, for his superiors, in order that they have something to amuse themselves with when they return triumphant to the base.

In the bungalow, in the bed, under the white covers, peace reigns. And now that the suffering soldier has stopped struggling, peace reigns outside too.

Nevertheless, a few silhouettes can be seen moving in the vast vagueness on the other side of the fence: the local inhabitants creeping towards their comrade who stands, as if impaled, on the frontier.

At first, Lucho feels something tickling him and is about to laugh or cry out. It's us, they whisper in his ear, and he grows quiet. All that separates them are the diamonds of interwoven wire, strong, solid, but in a way benign, for it allows the passage of straw, sacking, remnants and rags, an old jacket and a hat. In a twinkling Lucho has been transformed into a scarecrow, with straw covering his hands and a wig made from corn husks over half his face.

It suits him better than the scarecrow we dismantled, says a woman stuffing more straw into the sleeves. A case of robbing Peter to pay Paul, says a plump woman, creased up with laughter, and all the women applaud the bright idea of getting rid of their comrade in his capacity as Christ, or Prisoner, or even just plain Lucho, and replacing him with an inconspicuous scarecrow.

'Dressed like this, you'll scare off all the vultures, all the birds of evil omen.'

Wait, says a fourth woman and goes off in search of something, which she soon finds among the piles of rubbish. They're strips of silver paper that she places on the scarecrow's shoulders as if they were golden stripes. Epaulettes. Now he looks like the Major, one woman shouts, and they all burst into hysterical laughter.

'They can't touch him now!'

Under a roof, between four walls, just a few yards from Operation Scarecrow, Operation Between-the-sheets is enjoying a resurgence or reprise. This time the isolation appears less absolute and we hear certain exclamations, uttered falteringly and breathlessly:

'Your weapons are the best!'

'Your training is superior!'

'With us you will face/the greatest of life's challenges!'

'Yourself!'

'Yourself!'

'Us!'

The Manual has clearly been causing havoc in the bed. To make matters worse, it appears to have secondary effects, like dumdum bullets, attracting somewhat unsavoury energies.

Snug in their cocoon as twin silkworms, the lovers don't hear the knock at the door. Then more loud knocking is heard and the Señora, somewhat startled, sticks her nose out, clutching the sheets to her. Who is it? she manages to say and for answer she sees María march into the room carrying a tray.

'I've brought your supper, Señora. It's very late.'

'I don't want any supper, I didn't order any supper. You can go now.'

'Oh, I'll go, don't worry. But you owe me 53,000 for the roast chicken. I can't take it back.'

'I don't want any supper,' insists the Señora.

'It's just gone up to 55,000.'

'All right, leave it then, quickly, and draw the curtains. I'm suffocating in here.'

María doesn't notice the suspicious lump, making itself as flat as possible in the bed, blending in with the body of the bed's legitimate occupant. She leaves the tray and the plate of crisp, golden chicken at the Señora's feet and goes over to the French windows.

She can get stuffed for all I care, let her catch cold then, that'll teach her, María seems to be saying as she wrenches open the curtains, as if she'd like to tear them from their hangings.

The Señora takes advantage of the moment to give her beloved a little shove, indicating that he hide beneath the bed. He kisses her on the spot that happens to be nearest and, like Lucho, slides out from beneath the covers and disappears under the bed. Only it's not so simple for him, first he has to disentangle himself from the sheets. But it doesn't matter, he manages it and finds the secret tunnel. Meanwhile, the Señora has pulled out a fistful of notes which she holds out to María.

María counts the notes almost joyfully. Change, she says to herself, I've got some change, I'm going to make a killing on this. And she rushes off to do a deal.

20

The Señora has sacrificed her privacy to save Alfredi. Or to save herself, who knows. Everything that happens there is weird and vaguely disquieting, however inoffensive it may seem. Like children playing at war, with all the easy cruelty and naturalness of children. And to think that . . .

No. Why so much thinking? Thinking's bad for you, they'd told her.

This brief gust of reflection is suddenly interrupted by a cataclysmic vibration. The bed jumps as if shaken by an earthquake. It's the soldiers, in parade uniform and full war paint, who march in disciplined fashion through the French windows and into the room. The Señora is not afraid, not that afraid anyway. She realizes at once that the infantry have not been attracted to the foot of her bed by her rather sketchy ideas but by the dish of roast chicken. With a look of ravenous greed, they march straight for it. The Señora halts them with a look of her own and, defiantly, picks up the tray at her feet and slips it quickly under the bed, like a magician's sleight of hand which the soldiers spot, embarrassed. They beat an immediate retreat in the same formation as they advanced and, with an air of innocence, disappear back through the French windows into the night.

The shanty town dwellers feel no pity for the soldiers' hunger. They're at the fence again, making fun of the 101 dalmatians as they've taken to calling them. The people in the shanty town are eating chicken and as they throw the cleaned bones at the soldiers, they shout:

'Come on dalmatians, spotty dogs, mangy dogs, eat up. Eat up, dogs, and I hope the chicken bones splinter and choke you.'

'This is for the Major,' shouts one, tossing over a chicken leg.

The Señora is half-aware of this class struggle, of these contradictions in the system. But she feels like an overloaded computer. The alarm is sounding (and how!), an insidious whistling that obliges her to stop in the middle of an idea, to stop thinking and slide down in the bed and die a little, just enough to be able to see on the screen of her mind a stream of information flashing by too swiftly for her to register. One after another, the pages of her memory turn at top speed, leaving barely the trace of a sentence, a word, before they're erased to give way to another and another and another. The alarm sounds, she stops, doesn't think about what is possible – thinking is dangerous, to remember fatal, says a voice inside her, though she knows that, in fact, the contrary might be true.

Even the oversized TV screen can be capricious in Las Ranas country club or, more precisely, in bungalow 37B, in the extreme north of the grounds, the bungalow with which we're concerned. There, the screen, which for long hours has been filled by tiny dancing points of colour, bathing the room in aquatic light, seems to have suddenly come back to life, without being asked, without anyone switching it on. Now the Señora in her bed can watch, in amazement, a sort of replay of the scene that she herself had experienced not half an hour before, complete with military parade.

115

The rebel army is advancing – the blacking on their faces is for camouflage purposes, explains the announcer's voice – and this time they're not advancing on a mere biped, plucked for the occasion and done to a turn, on the contrary.

'The rebels, billeted in Las Ranas, are ready to march on the capital if their demands are not met,' explains the voice. 'The people have gathered outside the gates of the barracks to demand the unconditional surrender of the rebel soldiers. In the corridors of power in the government and in the Ministry of Defence it is said that the matter will go no further, but others fear bloody confrontations between the people and the rebel troops.'

The Señora who, before, used to complain about the television, stares at the screen, fascinated. Now, the part of her that obeys the orders not to think feels rather pleased: at last she's going to be a witness to history and not, as usually happens, a mere puppet; the part that doesn't want to think relaxes, but it's far from being the best or even the most valid part of her. The other part of her feels desperate and is on the point of hurling a shoe at the screen that depicts the soldiers life-size, almost flesh-and-blood real.

A hand restrains her. It's Alfredi who, without her noticing, has come in through the open window.

116 In fact, it's Alfredi in yet another of his incarnations, although the Señora has no difficulty recognizing him because she recognizes the touch of his hand on her arm. But for the others, one hopes, he will preserve his anonymity behind the heavy camouflage paint applied to his face. He looks rather like Al Jolson all blacked up, with a thick layer of boot polish slapped on haphazardly. He's wearing a ragbag of a uniform, the uniform – kepi, shirt and trousers – that was stolen from the guard the night before, with the addition of a few very ostentatious epaulettes and fake stripes. A few medals too, made out of tin, although the ensemble as a whole looks real enough for it not to seem like a disguise from a distance.

With his saluting hand, soldier Alfredi restrains the Señora and the Señora allows him to do so. He stands to attention and, addressing the giant screen, roars:

'Regiment. Atten . . . shun! Well done, men. You've carried out the manoeuvre to perfection. Tomorrow will be a day of glory. At . . . ease!'

Astonishing though it may seem, the troops obey these orders, orders that reach them from the other side of the unreal world in which they are immersed.

Wielding a poker instead of a baton, Alfredi says temptingly:

'It's chow time, soldiers. Forward, march!'

The troops obey. They shuffle sideways to form two packed double columns and proceed to goosestep out from the television screen, appearing in the room on either side of it.

Only Major Vento remains voluntarily trapped in the screen. He grows larger, filling all the available space, and speaks into the microphone:

'We are going to safeguard the true values of our Fatherland, values that have been threatened by the rank ineptitude of my comrades in arms. In our glorious regiment billeted in Las Ranas, we are all men of action, not penpushers! And we are ready to act. Any day now we will march on the capital and remember this: we do not feel cast down by the enemy, rather we feel cheered. We intend to restore military dignity by exalting the supreme values of discipline and courage.'

The Señora can bear no more, perhaps she can't bear the invasion of the soldiery gathered round her bed either, and she finally hurls a shoe at the screen.

'And now for the break,' says the announcer's voice and immediately the advertisements come on.

Harmony pasties, Spring Sun instant stew, croissants from Ibn Emir Sánchez.

There's some unrest among the soldiers, who are no longer standing in the strict formation in which they entered the room.

'Men, dismiss! It's chow time, soldiers!' roars Colonel Alfredi. 'Lay down your weapons,' he tells them, pointing to the bed where the Señora lies, curled up into an (almost) invisible ball.

The soldiers, greedy and starving, hurriedly leave their guns on the bed. They don't want to be carrying any excess baggage at chow time. And they run out through the French windows towards the smoke drifting over from a barbecue in the shanty town.

As they stampede out, the soldiers do not seem surprised that the chain-link fence has disappeared, doubtless cut down by the hordes of anonymous vandals. The prisoner they'd left tied up there has disappeared along with the fence. The soldiers are in no state to register changes in the terrain: now they can only respond to the call of their stomachs and there, on a huge barbecue, which is in fact part of the chain-link fence, a couple of tempting hindquarters are turning, golden and crackling. It's horse flesh but how are they to know that?

The sound of cheerful folk music comes gradually nearer, as if to keep time with the clattering jaws. Someone from the shanty town has gone to get his concertina and the music becomes a tango, homely and affectionate. Indifferent to the mountains of food available, Alfredi goes calmly over to the Señora on the bed and holds out his hand to her.

'Shall we dance?'

Guitars have now joined the concertina which has pretensions to being a bandoneon. But it's clear that not all the hands in the shanty town are busy making music because a few emerge once more from the subterranean depths of the Señora's bed and make off with the guns.

The only hand the Señora sees is that of her beloved, but she's not sure she should take that hand, worried that it might have gone over to the other side in exchange for the stripes he's wearing now a little higher up on his cuff.

'Come on, let's dance,' insists her versatile lover.

The Señora takes his hand, but that's all, and tries to pull him down towards the bed.

'No,' he says, 'standing up.'

'Oh, not vertical, not yet,' she pleads.

'Yes, vertical. With your head held high.'

'I need a bit more time.'

'Now is the time.'

'Wait. I want to understand. I'm afraid.'

'Get up. Only death can cure your fear of death. It's not worth it. It's better to be alive and moving, while you can. We have to celebrate.'

And to prove it he rips off his epaulettes and uses the white bedspread to clean his face as best he can.

'No more cabbie, colonel, doctor or madman, I can at last go back to being me.'

'And who are you?' asks the Señora, slightly alarmed.

'Me? Well, let's just say I'm the one who came to put an end to this whole farce. Or at least to the players in the farce. As far as possible.'

The musicians have come into the room. He gets up on the bed and takes her in his arms. She stands up without a protest and together on the bed they begin to dance a tango which, in one graceful step, takes them to the floor to become, in turn, polka, foxtrot, salsa, samba, cumbia, calypso, and they dance and dance while the music flows merrily and seamlessly on.

120 Now it's a waltz and the Señora's filmy white nightdress flies and whirls, cleansing the air of the room.

Until, black and pernicious, the phone rings again.

Startled, the Señora stops in mid-twirl and her nightdress winds about her legs.

'Let's not answer it,' she begs Alfredi, holding him close.

'All right,' he says calmly.

The person at the other end of the line doesn't give up. The ringing drowns out the musicians. The Señora recovers from her fear:

'I *am* going to answer it after all. I don't want to be an ostrich ever again, I want to know who it is.'

'But we already know,' Alfredi says gently as he whirls her towards the window and out into the grounds. And there she sees the whole shanty town approaching, carrying the guns that were on the bed, laughing like crazy things, carrying the rifles any old how, as if it were carnival time.

It would seem that the TV wants to join the party too, for the image of a giant cake appears on the screen, getting larger and larger as the camera zooms in on it, until it's one huge closeup that looks more like cloud or like foam than meringue.

Indifferent to the general merriment, the telephone goes on ringing while, in the background, the soldiers are seeing off the last scraps of meat. The meat nearest the bone is best, they say, and the telephone rings on. The Señora at last goes over to answer it. A young girl from the shanty town, Patri apparently, gets there before her and pulls out the plug. It's one of those modern telephones, round in shape, and Patri throws it to her companions as if it were a rubber ball.

'Ouch!' shouts the voice from the phone.

And that's the last thing it shouts, because the ball is flying now among the people from the shanty town. Some hit it with the butts of their rifles: Anyone for tennis? they shout. Others shunt it along the floor with the barrel: Anyone for golf? Let's play ring-around-the-roses, cry the youngest and they form an enormous circle about the weapons that are now piled on the ground.

The Señora and Alfredi are in the middle of the circle. There are shouts of victory and applause for both of them.

'Now the club is ours!' he says, stamping on the weapons.

'And the country?' asks she, ever the realist.

For Rodolfo Walsh
in memoriam